I0724787

Stone Warrior

Stone Warrior

Avril Sabine

Cracked Acorn Productions
Australia

Stone Warrior

Published by

Cracked Acorn Productions

PO Box 1365

Gympie, Queensland 4570

Australia

978-1-925131-12-3 (Kindle)

978-1-925617-44-3 (EPUB)

978-1-925131-13-0 (Print)

978-1-925131-16-1 (Printed in Australia)

Genre: Young Adult Urban Fantasy

Copyright 2014 © Avril Sabine

Cover design by Caitlyn Petersen

All rights reserved

*For my mum, a warrior more fierce than
Boudica when protecting her kids. When I
was growing up, I always knew she'd be in
the front lines of any battle I had to face.*

Seventeen-year-old Sydney and her parents have finally found something major they can't agree on. Hell will freeze over before they let her date Shawn. Sydney is not going to let that stop her. Even when her plans go astray and she accidentally frees Corrin, a Celtic warrior, from his stone imprisonment, she is still determined. Her and Shawn are destined for each other. Parents, ancient warriors and evil spirits will not keep them apart. Sydney and Shawn forever.

*

This story was written by an Australian author using Australian spelling.

Name Pronunciation

Like many names there is more than one way to pronounce the following ones. These are the pronunciations used in this story.

Corrin (koh-rin)
Lorcan (law-ken)
Orlaith (or-la)

Chapter One

Sydney's stomach churned. Fear and excitement twisted together as they entered yet another room in the museum. She slowed her steps so most of the class was now ahead of her and Chelsea. The curator stopped in front of a life sized stone statue and the two of them stayed at the back of the group. She checked out the Dark Age display and a smile slowly formed. This part of the exhibit was perfect. She turned towards Chelsea, whose grin matched her own.

"Here?" Chelsea nodded her head towards the statue as she spoke. She had bleached blond hair just past her shoulders, pale blue eyes and fair skin.

Sydney nodded. "In the area behind the statue. No one should see me if I hide in the shadows behind him." Her dark brown hair fell to her shoulders, almost black in colour. She had eyes a similar colour to her hair, an oval face and light brown skin.

Chelsea linked her arm with Sydney's. "Are you sure you want to do this? If you get caught your parents will ground you for the entire September school holidays. Two weeks of boredom. Besides, I need you to be my chauffeur. My parents said I could borrow their car when the sun no longer rises. So I'm not holding my breath. Which is unfair since your parents didn't even ground you that time you brought their car back with a dent."

"Yeah, but my sister wouldn't shut up about it. Now quit worrying. I won't get caught. Absolutely nothing will go wrong. The plan is perfect."

Chelsea continued to look sceptical. "You say that every time."

"You make it sound like none of my plans have worked. And they do. Anyway, this time's different. I've got it all figured out."

Chelsea sighed. "I really hope so. I want to go to the beach tomorrow. That'd be a perfect way to start the holidays." She fell silent when their teacher rounded on them with a glare.

Sydney glanced at Chelsea and rolled her eyes before turning her attention to the curator. He'd been talking away at the front of the group, gesturing to various areas around the room where illuminated display cabinets showed different items of a long dead society.

The curator indicated the stone statue he stood near. "And now we come to the highlight of our exhibition. This Celtic warrior's name has long been forgotten but his story is a legend that would make an epic movie. He is said to have stolen his brother's wife. The husband, unable to kill his own brother, turned him to stone. He sacrificed his unfaithful wife to create the spell. The woman died cursing them and said the spell would one day break and she'd have her revenge. A druid added his own guarantee. The spell would only end by a kiss from a virgin, in gratitude to the stone warrior for a service he had done. Once he is human again he will remain bound to her until he completes a great service for her."

Chelsea leaned close. "I wouldn't mind having him come to life."

Sydney laughed softly. "You'd be bored within a week."

Chelsea rolled her eyes. "Once. It was only once. Anyone would think I'd never been with a guy for longer than a week the way you go on about it. Besides, you can't talk. At least I've beaten your six week record." Another look of annoyance from their teacher ended her protests.

The curator took a step towards the students who stood restlessly in front of him. "So do we have a grateful virgin willing to give this stone warrior CPR?" A twitter of laughter travelled through the group as the museum curator glanced at each of them in turn. "None?"

Sydney raised her hand. "I'll give it a try."

The curator smiled. "You'll have to blow him a kiss. No touching the exhibits, I'm afraid."

"Now where's the fun in that?" Sydney asked.

"It wouldn't work anyway. You have to be a virgin," one of the boys in the class called out.

Sydney gestured towards him with her middle finger as she muttered to Chelsea, "You're right, a week was way too long. You should have dumped him after a day."

Chelsea grinned. "That certainly leaves you out, Justin."

"I'm not a girl," Justin said.

Chelsea's grin remained in place. "That's debatable."

Justin took several steps towards her. "You want–"

"Okay, calm down." The teacher stepped in front of Justin. "No fighting in the museum."

With a wink to her friend, Chelsea stepped away from Sydney and moved closer to Justin. "He started it."

"And now it's finished," the teacher said.

The curator moved forward. "If everyone will follow me, we have several more displays to look at."

"How can it be finished?" Chelsea demanded as she walked beside the teacher. "Finishing implies something was completed. This wasn't. Why should he get away with saying crap like that? I never do."

When everyone's attention was on Chelsea and Justin, Sydney slipped quietly into the shadow cast by the warrior. She stared at the back of the cloaked figure while she listened to the sounds of her class moving away, hoping no one could see her. His hair was tied at the nape of his neck, falling below his shoulders. She wondered what colour hair the original model had. Whoever he'd been, he would have been worm food centuries ago.

When the sounds of her classmates faded, Sydney started to step past the warrior. She paused and looked up at him. A glance around the room showed it was empty and she smiled, unable to resist. Besides, the curator shouldn't have asked who was willing if he was just going to tell them no.

"Thank you for your help." Her hand rested on his

arm as she leaned towards him and pressed her lips against the smooth, cool stone of his cheek. "Without your help my plan might have failed." She took a step backwards. As she was about to move away, the lights went out sending the room into complete darkness.

Sydney froze. A rush of wind swirled around her and she reached towards the statue to steady herself. Her hand met warm skin and she inhaled sharply as she wondered who was in the room with her. Had she been turned around in the dark? She was almost certain she hadn't moved. She took a large step backwards, her hand falling away. In the darkness she heard voices call out from other display rooms. Some sounded scared, others laughed nervously and several called out for everyone to remain where they were. Another voice said the backup generator should kick in at any moment. Yet it remained dark. She kept still when all she wanted to do was run. The last thing she needed was to crash into something, or someone, in the dark. She took a cautious step backwards.

Over and over she silently told herself to remain calm as she fumbled in her pocket for her house keys, which had a slim torch on the chain. Relief filled her as she pulled out the torch, turning it on. The narrow beam was pointed at the industrial carpet under her feet. Her relief was short lived. She shone the light on a pair of leather boots and slowly moved the beam upwards to see woollen breeches. The figure wore a striped cloak, a long sword hung from a bronze chain on his right and his tunic was embroidered. The light caught on the brooch that held the cloak at one shoulder. The light had also caused gold jewellery to glitter on his fingers, arms, wrists, neck and ears as it had travelled up his body.

Sydney's heart raced as she took a step backwards. Her mouth opened, but not a single sound escaped. Escape! That's what she needed to do. There was no way a Celtic warrior could be standing in front of her. Maybe it was a terrorist attack and they'd released some kind of drug into the air-conditioning to make people see things. She wasn't about to wait around to find out for certain. She spun and started to run from the room.

"Wait. Who are you?"

Sydney shone the narrow beam of light behind her. The warrior followed, a long oval shield held in one hand. She sped up, forcing her legs to obey. Her heart raced faster, her breath caught in her throat and she realised she was almost sobbing. Where was everyone? Why had she wanted to leave the group?

It had been a great plan. All she'd had to do was hide until her class was out of view and then head for the bus stop. Shawn was waiting for her to meet him at his place. It had been foolproof. How had it gone wrong?

Maybe her parents were right. She should forget all about Shawn. Find a boyfriend they'd like. She burst out the main doors. The bright sunlight made her blink as she stopped to let her eyes adjust while taking in large gulps of air. The noise of engines competed with the sound of cascading water from a nearby fountain.

People hurried by. No one looked in her direction. Some were sitting on benches, gazes focused on mobile phones and one leaned back on his hands, eyes closed, face towards the sun, as he listened to his music. Everything looked normal, right down to an empty wrapper being blown across the concrete in front of her.

Chapter Two

"Who are you?"

Sydney spun to see the warrior who had followed her outside. She took an unsteady step away. "Who are you?"

"Corrin."

Sydney momentarily closed her eyes. She was hearing things as well as seeing things. Now she was talking to her hallucination. She had to go. Shawn was waiting for her. She bet he wouldn't be able to see Corrin. She turned away and hurried towards the bus stop. Maybe if she ignored him he'd disappear. Keeping her gaze on her destination, she watched a bus pull away as another one arrived.

"Wait." Corrin put his hand on her shoulder and turned her to face him.

Sydney pulled away from him. "You're not real."

"What?"

A kid that was around ten-years-old ran over to them. "Awesome. Are you in some sort of medieval group? Can anyone join?" He reached out to touch the edge of Corrin's striped cloak. "Can I join? Can I use your sword? Can you show me how to use it?"

A woman raced after the boy, one hand holding her straw hat on her head, and grabbed his hand. She muttered sorry as she pulled him away, scolding him. He didn't go quietly.

"He saw you." Sydney stared at Corrin.

"Why would he not?"

Sydney couldn't answer. Instead she stared at him. He had medium brown hair tied at the nape of his neck, bronze highlights where the sun hit it and a square jaw. Confusion showed in his dark brown eyes. Across his right cheek was a faint scar and numerous ones on his hands and neck. She wondered if there were more scars hidden by his clothes.

"Who are you?"

"Sydney."

"Sydney?" The confusion remained in his eyes.

"Yeah, I know. Stupid name. It's a city. But Mum thought it was cute. Her name is Victoria and Dad is Malcolm. His nickname is Mal, you know, kind of like the city Melbourne. Or that's what my mum thinks. And she named my sister Adelaide. It's-" She broke off as she realised she was babbling. Momentarily closing her eyes she mentally called herself an idiot. Preschoolers knew about stranger danger. "Look, I've got somewhere to be. Plans. Quit following me, okay?"

Corrin frowned. "Okay?"

Sydney nodded and turned to stride towards the bus stop again. She sighed heavily as Corrin fell into step beside her. "You can't come with me. Find something else to do." She had no clue what was going on, but shortly it wouldn't matter. She'd be on the bus and out of here, on the way to Shawn's. Once she was on the bus she could forget all about this episode.

"Sydney. Where are we?"

"Brisbane."

"Where is this Brisbane? I have never heard of it. And this place." His hand waved in a vague circle. "What magic is all this?"

Sydney stopped suddenly to stare at him. "There is a logical explanation. Magic isn't real." She wasn't sure if she answered him or reminded herself. "Just don't follow me. I can't deal with this. I've got too many other problems."

"We are bound together until I perform a great service for you."

Sydney raised her hands as if to push him away. "Oh no. No way. I don't need this." She took a step backwards. "Just… I don't know. Anything. Do anything. Go anywhere. Just stay away from me. Okay?"

"What is this okay?"

Sydney shook her head. "Forget it." She turned away as she heard the bus arrive and ran towards it. Her foot on the bus step, she turned back to Corrin who had followed. There was nothing she could do for him, not if she wanted to see Shawn. "Good luck."

"Sydney!"

Ignoring him, she paid her fare and found a seat. Behind her she heard the bus driver refuse to let Corrin board and she breathed a sigh of relief as they started to pull away. She sat in a seat by herself and looked out the window at Corrin, who stared back at her. A touch of guilt filled her. It wasn't like he was a stray puppy she could take home. Actually, she couldn't have taken him home even then. The last one she'd brought home her parents had taken to the RSPCA. She didn't think they'd accept a Celtic warrior.

She leaned back on the vinyl seat and closed her eyes. Celtic warrior! What on earth was she thinking? The entire encounter had been one moment of madness after another. Maybe the stress of year twelve was getting to her. Sydney's eyes flew open. Her skin felt like it was shrinking. She looked down at her bare arms. They looked exactly the same yet the skin felt as if it continued to tighten. Her stomach did a back flip and her head began to pound. The bus stopped and the sensation eased. When the bus lurched forward again, Sydney pressed the back of her hand against her nose as she felt it start to run. A splash of bright red blood formed on her hand.

"Here, luv." A woman across the aisle handed her a crumpled tissue.

Sydney pressed it against her nose as nausea hit her and her bones felt like they were being compressed, her skin paling before her eyes. Her skin seemed half a dozen sizes too small as she staggered to her feet, stumbling to the front of the bus. "I have to get off."

"Two minutes to the next stop." The bus driver didn't even glance in her direction.

"I have to get off." Sydney tried to contain the hysteria that filled her voice, but it was impossible. "Let me off." She tried not to look at the bright red spreading across the tissue she held against her nose.

The bus driver continued to watch the crowded road ahead. "Sit down. Next stop is two minutes."

"I'm going to be sick," Sydney wailed.

The bus lurched to a stop and the door slid open. She didn't wait, but was on the footpath in seconds, hearing several cars sounding their horns. She leaned against a metal light post, grasping the cold smooth metal. It felt arctic against her burning hand. She pressed her forehead against the coldness, a roaring in her ears making the world fade. She tried to think, but the only thought that would form clearly was, I'm going to die.

As quickly as it had begun, it started to ease until she was left clinging weakly to the light post, her skin no longer feeling like it was on fire and tightening around her bones. Her legs trembled and she was tempted to slide to the ground.

"Sydney!"

She looked up to see Corrin run towards her, blood streaking his face where he'd wiped it away from his nose. Her stomach did another back flip as her mouth dropped open. She shook her head as he came to a stop in front of her. "No. Oh no. Please no." Still shaking her head, she took another step away from him.

Corrin reached out towards her. "Sydney-"

She dodged his hand. "No. I have plans for today. And they don't include you." She watched a man run into someone as he tried to give her and Corrin a wide berth. A glance around showed the crowded footpath was filled with people who eyed them warily as they kept their distance. She sighed heavily. The last thing she needed was to draw this kind of attention. What if someone who knew her parents saw her? She reached out and grabbed Corrin's hand. "Come on. We can't stand around here." Not that she had any idea where to take him.

Spying a narrow alley, she led him down it, avoiding rubbish bins and crushed cardboard boxes. She leaned against a concrete wall and crossed her arms as she stared up at Corrin. He had to be close to six foot. "What am I going to do with you?" She looked down at the crumpled tissue in her hand, the blood already darkening as it dried. She struggled to accept the impossible. Her gaze was drawn to Corrin again. He was real and a hell of a lot bigger than a stray puppy. When he didn't speak, she asked again, "What am I supposed to do with you?"

"I must serve you until we are no longer bound."

"What does that mean?" She threw the tissue into the closest bin and wished she had a clean one to offer Corrin. She put her hands behind her back and pressed them against the rough concrete wall so she wouldn't be tempted to clean him up.

Corrin's hand went to the hilt of his sword. "You

are more than my chieftain while we are bound. Anything you ask of me, if it is in my power to do so, I will."

"I don't want this."

"Then why did you release me?"

Sydney couldn't help laughing. "Someone told me not to. Anyway, I didn't think it was real. Magic isn't real."

Corrin grinned. "Lorcan always said I would take on an army if someone said it could not be done."

"Who is Lorcan?"

Corrin's smile faded. "We were fostered together with our tribe's chieftain. He was a brother to me." Corrin turned away to face the opening of the alley, his voice dropping. "I failed him."

"How?"

"I promised to bring Orlaith back. I never should have listened to her. I should have gagged her." Corrin turned to meet her gaze. "She was a viper. She spoke lies like they were the truth of the gods."

Sydney opened her mouth to ask more questions then quickly closed it. She wasn't getting caught up in his stories. She had to figure out a way to get rid of him. And quickly or she wouldn't get to see Shawn today. Her parents would be home at five and they'd expect her there too. "How do we get rid of this bound together thing?" Sydney pulled her phone out of her pocket and checked the time. Ten-thirty. If she wasn't at Shawn's by midday he wouldn't be there. "We've got an hour to sort it out." She returned her phone to her pocket.

"Performing a great service will take days or even months to complete. Unless your life is in danger and I save you."

"Sweet. I can deal with that. I'll run out into the traffic and you can pull me back. You let me die and I'll haunt you." Sydney headed for the opening of the alley.

Chapter Three

Corrin grabbed her arm and pulled her back to him. He shook his head. "It does not work like that. That would not be saving you. That would be preventing you from something you wish to do."

"But I don't want to kill myself." Sydney frowned. "Hang on. Preventing me from something I wish to do? You mean you'd let a friend kill themselves?"

"Better to die by your own sword than be captured by the enemy and tortured."

"You'd kill yourself?" Sydney shook her head and held up her hand. "Forget it. I don't want to know. Well I do, but we don't have time. What's the quickest way to deal with this?"

"There is no quick way."

Realizing Corrin still held her arm, Sydney drew away from him. "This is impossible. I can't take you with me to my boyfriend's place. And I certainly can't take you home. My parents would kill me."

"I would not let them."

Sydney frowned until she realised Corrin had taken her words literally. "Not kill me as in dead. But, well ground me or something. I'd be in a lot of trouble."

"Once you explain they will understand."

Sydney laughed, no humour evident. "Yeah, and then they'd cart me off to the psych ward. Just what I need." She eyed his sword and shield. "Do you have to carry those around? Can't you get rid of them?" She gestured towards the sword and shield.

Corrin looked shocked. "A warrior goes nowhere without his weapons."

"Not in this century. Warriors are obsolete."

"Obsolete?"

"No longer in existence. Extinct. Gone. I don't know. Get yourself a dictionary or something and read it."

"I cannot read."

"Really?" Sydney stared at him for a moment. He didn't seem bothered by that fact. "I guess things were different in the Dark Ages." She took a deep breath and slowly let it out. "Forget all that for now. You keep getting me sidetracked." She held up her hand when a look of confusion crossed his face again and he started to speak. "Forget it. All I want to talk about is how to deal with this mess. And stop giving me that 'I wouldn't have a clue' look. It's starting to annoy me."

"If more of your words made sense I would understand what you were saying."

Sydney glared at him. It wasn't her fault he came from some dead century. "How far apart can we be? Was that simple enough for you?"

Corrin slid his hand inside his cloak and rested it high on his left arm and muttered, "Epona give me patience."

"Who is Epona?"

"My goddess. She is the protector of horses." He slid the edge of his cloak back, drawing up the short sleeve of his tunic to reveal a tattoo on his upper arm. The swirling geometric design included a stylised horse.

Sydney started to ask him another question then stopped and glared at him. "You're doing it again. Stop sidetracking me. Now how far apart can we be?"

"I do not know."

"If it's not far you better get used to nosebleeds because I'm not sharing a bathroom with you."

"What–"

"Quiet." Sydney pulled out her phone that was

vibrating. She glanced at the screen before she answered it. "Chelz! Please tell me no one has noticed I'm missing."

"No. Oh Sydney, you can't imagine what's going on here. There are police everywhere."

Sydney swore. "I should have thought about that. He's going to have to ditch his shield. It's like asking people to look at us. No one carries a shield around these days, do they? And it's over a metre long."

"Ah, Sydney, are you okay?"

"No. I'm not. I planned this out perfectly. No one in their right mind would think of factoring in a Celtic warrior."

"You know? How did you find out the statue was stolen? The backup generator didn't work. It was dark for ages and no one could use their phones. Everything failed. No electricity, no phone coverage, not even security cameras. Only torches. Then all of a sudden it was all working again."

"Chelz can we forget about all that for a minute? I still need to get to Shawn's."

"Are you still here? Where abouts are you? I'm in the bathroom. Should we meet up? Why aren't you on your way to Shawn's place?"

Sydney groaned and leaned back against the concrete wall. She closed her eyes so she didn't have to look at Corrin who was busy checking out one of the compacted cardboard boxes. She swore again. "You are not going to believe a word I say, but seriously, it wasn't my fault. Well, maybe it was kinda. But magic doesn't exist. Does it Chelz?"

"Ahh… no?"

"See. Even you know."

"I do?"

"Yep. So why does it?"

"It does?"

"Of course it does. So how do I get rid of him?"

"You know, Sydney, it'd help if you started from the beginning. I have no idea what you're talking about."

"Never mind. I'll figure it out."

"Just don't get grounded. I want to go to the beach tomorrow. Remember?"

Sydney eyed Corrin, trying to imagine him in board shorts. She quickly emptied her mind and reminded herself of Shawn. "I've got to go. I'll call you later, Chelz."

"Okay. But don't go doing anything stupid."

As Sydney slid her phone into her pocket she thought it was probably too late for that advice. The image of Corrin in board shorts just wouldn't leave her mind. That was it. She needed real clothes for him. That was why she kept thinking of board shorts. She pushed away from the wall. "We've got to buy you some clothes. And ditch the glitter and weapons."

Corrin frowned at her. "I am not leaving my things in a ditch. They would be stolen."

"Not a ditch. Just somewhere. You know. Drop it off. Put it somewhere." It was Sydney's turn to frown. "Oh never mind. Wait there." She strode to the end of the alley and looked around. She spotted a discount store across the road. It would have to do. She turned back to Corrin who had followed her. "Wait here. How much more simple can I say that? Don't move from here. Okay?"

Corrin nodded and crossed his arms over his chest as he looked down at her. "You will be back?"

"As if I have a choice," Sydney muttered as she hurried out of the alley before glancing up and down the road. The light at the corner was red so she ran through the stopped traffic, barely making the opposite footpath in time. Her skin tightened and she looked back to where she'd come from. All she could see in the alleyway was shadows. But he had to still be there. She didn't have a nosebleed yet.

It was an effort to concentrate on what she needed to buy. She gathered a black backpack and an extra large t-shirt since she didn't know his size. After grabbing two large striped plastic bags, and a travel pack of tissues that she opened when she reached the other end of the store, she headed for the checkout. Tucking the bloody tissue into a pocket of her jeans as she fished out her coin purse, her foot tapped as she waited for her turn at the checkout. She grunted in answer when the checkout operator asked if she was having a good day. She was tempted to answer absolutely awful, but kept her mouth shut and used her keycard when the items were tallied up. It was a relief to run back across the road and into the alley.

"Here." She handed the green t-shirt to Corrin and pulled out a tissue for him. "For the blood," she said when he stared at the white square. "And put all your jewellery in this." She held up the backpack.

He eyed the item she still held. "All of it?"

Sydney's gaze roamed his body. "Most of it at least. Give me your shield and sword so I can put them in the rainbow bags."

"You will not leave them in a ditch?"

Sydney shook her head and took the items Corrin reluctantly handed her. "And your cloak too."

He watched as she packed his sword, shield and cloak into the red, blue and white striped bag. She slid another one over the top since his gear protruded from the bag. "What are you going to do with it?"

"Can you hurry up? Take your shirt off and put that one on. I haven't got all day." Sydney pulled her phone out and looked at the time. She swore. "I'm not going to make it. Do you know how much effort it took to plan this day? And you ruined it in a matter of seconds." One hand went to her hip as she glared at him. "Come on. You do know how to dress yourself, don't you?"

Corrin grinned. "If I said no, would you do it for me?"

Sydney rolled her eyes. Guys were all the same. "How old are you?" He had to be at least several years older than her.

Corrin shrugged as he pulled his tunic over his head and put it inside the backpack.

Chapter Four

Sydney stared at the scars that criss-crossed his body. "How did you get them?" When he looked confused, she added, "The scars."

Corrin pulled the t-shirt over his head. "Battle."

Sydney continued to stare at his arms. "I should have bought you a long sleeve shirt. You look like a cutter."

"A what?"

She shook her head. "Never mind. Can you hurry up? It's taking you ages to get your jewellery off."

Corrin eyed the zip on the backpack when the only jewellery he had left on was a gold torc around his neck and a single bronze armband. He watched as Sydney zipped it up for him then had to open and close the bag several times himself.

"Come on." She grabbed hold of the rainbow bags, which he instantly took from her. "Fine. I won't help.

But hurry up. We need to ditch this stuff at my house. We can't carry it around everywhere."

Corrin followed Sydney to the bus shelter. "You said you would not leave my things in a ditch."

She ran her fingers down the board as she read the timetable. "I'm not… oh never mind."

"I do mind. You are not leaving my things in a ditch."

"Quiet for a minute. This is our bus." She pulled him towards the vehicle that had just arrived, not wanting to miss it. "Hurry up." She paid the fare and dragged him to a seat towards the rear that was surrounded by empty seats. "Sit down." When she saw he was about to speak, she added, "And be quiet." She pushed him towards the window and slid onto the seat after him.

"Can I speak now?"

"No."

"Why not?"

"Didn't I just say you couldn't speak? Seriously, how hard is that to understand?"

"What are we on? What makes it move?"

"Shh." Sydney glanced around, but no one seemed to have heard. "Didn't you say you had to do what I asked? Then I'm asking you to shut up. At least until we get to my place."

Corrin stared at her a moment before he turned his attention to the window. Sydney waited to see if he would speak again, but he remained silent. She continued to watch him as he stared out the window. What was she going to do with him? Talk about impossible situations. And what would happen if there was too much distance between them? Worse than a nosebleed? Worse than feeling like her body was being compressed in on itself? She shuddered. There had to be a way to break their connection. The school holidays started tomorrow and she had plans. They didn't include hanging out with a guy who should have been dead centuries ago.

When they arrived at their destination Sydney still hadn't figured out a solution. She hurried off the bus, pulling Corrin behind her. He shook her hand off his wrist and stopped to watch the bus pull away.

"Can I talk now?"

"If you have to."

"What were we in the belly of?" He gestured towards the bus that turned the corner at the end of the street.

Sydney shook her head. "Forget it. Come on." She headed in the opposite direction the bus had taken.

"Why will you not answer my questions?"

"Because they can't be answered in a couple of

sentences. Just think of it as," she paused, trying to think of something to compare it to. "A horseless carriage. Or hang on, you lot had chariots, didn't you? Well, it's like a horseless chariot."

"Horses smell a lot better."

"That's debateable."

"What-"

"Oh quit with the questions. You're worse than a four-year-old." She turned the corner and crossed the road. "No wonder I don't do babysitting." She glanced towards Corrin when he made no reply. She ignored the twinge of guilt she felt. He'd just have to get used to it. She didn't have time to teach him about the modern world. And even if she did have the time, she had no clue how to explain half the things that were catching his attention. She turned up her driveway and walked around to the back of the house, fishing her keys out of her pocket as she walked. She reminded herself once again that she needed to have a key cut for the front door. Since she'd moved into her sister's old room the front door was the closest entrance to her new room.

She paused at the open door. "Don't touch anything in here, okay?"

"I still do not understand this okay word."

"Do I look like a bloody dictionary?"

Corrin shrugged. "Since I have no idea what a dictionary looks like I cannot answer that question."

"Shut up," Sydney growled as she stepped inside and waited for him to follow. She slammed the door closed, but it didn't make her feel any better. This was not how her day was meant to be. She strode to her bedroom and opened her built-in wardrobe. "Put your gear in here." She eyed him up and down. "And do you have any other weapons? The last thing we need is for you to end up in jail."

Corrin pulled a dagger from his boot and Sydney added it to the pile. She quickly used her ensuite and then showed him how the bathroom worked. Next she pulled the chair out from her desk and told Corrin to sit. Dropping onto her bed she lay back against her pillows as she dialled Shawn's number.

"What?"

"I can't get there by midday."

"I'm not waiting around. I already told you that."

Sydney glared at Corrin who was investigating a pencil he'd found on her desk. "I know. I was just letting you know things didn't work out like I planned."

"You can come over tomorrow. But not before eleven. I won't be awake."

"I promised to take Chelsea to the beach tomorrow."

"And what about your promise to spend this afternoon with me?"

"I'm sorry, Shawn. I did try, but-"

"Look, this sneaking around is a drama. I don't need dramas. They-"

Sydney broke in frantically. "Sunday. What about Sunday?"

There was a pause before Shawn answered. "Not till eleven."

Sydney counted to five before she replied, trying to control the relief she felt. "Okay. I'll see you then." She closed her eyes when Shawn said goodbye and disconnected. Letting her phone fall onto the bed beside her, she took several calming breaths. It didn't help. She had to figure out how to see Shawn on Sunday. Without Corrin. She felt the bed sink and the warmth of a body against her hip. Her eyes flew open.

"Is there a problem?"

"Didn't I tell you to sit and stay?"

"Do you want me to bark too?"

Sydney glared at him. "The only problem I currently have is you. I had plans for today and you ruined them."

"Can I help you sort your plans out?"

"You're the reason my plans were ruined."

Corrin took hold of her hand. "I am sorry."

Sydney stared at her hand in his. The warmth of his skin and the roughness of his palm reminded her he was real. She raised her gaze to meet his. She had no clue what to do with him. She'd been completely focused on how to get rid of him. The feeling of guilt she'd been continually suppressing flared up again and she pulled her hand away from his. "Why did you do it?"

"Do what?"

"Steal your brother's wife." She tried to think of the name he'd told her earlier. "Lorcan. Why did you steal Lorcan's wife?"

Corrin stared at her, quiet for a change. Just when Sydney thought he wouldn't answer, he spoke. "I thought I was protecting her. When she ran away, I promised Lorcan I would bring her back. I should never have listened to her. She seemed so distressed. I could not help believing everything she told me." He reached out and ran a finger from the corner of her eye and down her cheek. "Could you cry tears of lies?"

Sydney stared up at Corrin. She wanted to wrap her arms around him and reassure him, but she held herself still. She swallowed and tried to speak. It came out as a whisper. "No."

He took her hand again. "I saw it in Lorcan's eyes when he caught us. Every word she had spoken was a lie. I tried to explain to him, but he said I should have known better. That I should never have believed anyone over him. He was right. We were raised together. I should have known not to believe what she said. I wish I could tell him he was right."

"I'm sorry." She rested her free hand over the one that held hers. "What happens when we're no longer bound? Do you get to go back to your time?"

"I do not know, but I think not."

"Oh." She looked away. How would it feel to be trapped in stone for centuries only to be released by someone who kept trying to get rid of you? To know that everyone you had once known was now dead. Her guilt increased but was quickly swamped by annoyance. This wasn't her fault. Not really. All she'd done was kiss a statue. Nothing should have happened. At the most she should have got into trouble for touching one of the exhibits. She pulled away, sliding past him to get off her bed.

Corrin rose to face her. "If I am to remain in your world I need to learn. To ask questions. Everything is strange."

Thoughts, feelings, words flashed through her mind, but she was unable to speak any of them. Not without sounding heartless or getting too personal. She needed to keep her distance. He'd be gone as soon as she could figure out how to break their bond. "Come on. We need to get you more clothes." She stared at him a moment longer. "And board shorts. I *am* going to the beach tomorrow." She strode from the room, not waiting to see if he followed. By the time she reached the back door, he was at her side.

Chapter Five

Sydney dropped the shopping bags onto the floor of her built-in wardrobe, with the rest of Corrin's gear. She returned to her laptop she'd turned on the moment she'd entered the room and went onto the internet. Within minutes she had a documentary on how cars worked and plugged in headphones. She showed Corrin how to play and pause the program and how to use the headphones.

"Now stay in here. Quietly. My parents will freak if they find you in my room. And if you get hungry, there's more snack food in one of the shopping bags I put in my wardrobe. But don't get crumbs everywhere." She looked towards her door at the sound of voices. "Quiet. They're here."

She stepped out of her room and closed the door behind her, glad this was a normal habit. Taking a deep breath she reminded herself there was no way her parents would know she'd accidentally set free a Celtic warrior and stashed him in her bedroom. Not unless she slipped up and told them.

Sydney stood at the start of the hallway, the front door to her back as she watched her parents walk side by side down the hallway, her mum waving a piece of paper at her dad who shook his head. She smiled as she listened to them argue. Her mum designed jewellery, her dad made it. That was how they'd met. She slowly followed behind them, her steps quiet on the carpet. She wondered, not for the first time, if they were disappointed that neither of their daughters had inherited their artistic talents. Her older sister, Adelaide, was a secretary in a doctor's office. As far from artistic as one could get. And the best she could do, was draw stick figures.

Victoria, her mum, looked back up the hallway and smiled at her. "Adelaide rang. Her and," she clicked her fingers several times as she frowned. "What is his name?" She shook her head. "Doesn't matter. They'll be here for dinner tomorrow night."

"Evan." Sydney supplied the name of Adelaide's boyfriend. "I'm going to the beach tomorrow with Chelsea. It's the first day of the school holidays. I need the car."

"As long as you're back by six. No, better make that

five. And I need the car in the morning. We need groceries." Victoria turned to her husband. "Can you get them in the morning, Mal?"

Malcolm nodded. "I thought you were going to ask Sydney to cook tomorrow night? Five doesn't give her much time."

"Will you love?" Victoria glanced at Sydney before she dumped her bag and several pages of designs on the island bench that sat in the middle of the kitchen.

"Again? I cooked last time we had Evan over." Sydney slid one of the stools out from the island bench and dropped onto it. She pulled a design over to look at the drawing, rubbing at the skin on her arms that felt too tight to fit over her bones.

"That's because your mum can't cook." Malcolm eyed the carton of eggs and loaf of bread his wife took from the fridge. "And eggs on toast don't count."

Victoria grabbed a bowl from an overhead cupboard. "Eggs are good for you. Plenty of vitamins." She turned to Sydney. "So can you cook, love?"

"Can I invite a friend to dinner then?" Sydney pushed the designs away from her, trying to ignore the tightness of her skin.

"Chelsea is always welcome," Victoria said.

"It's not Chelsea."

Malcolm paused in the action of putting a frypan on the hotplate. "It isn't Shawn, is it? We're not going to change our mind about that boy."

Sydney shook her head. "No. Corrin. You've never met him."

"What's he like?" Victoria put a bowl of eggs next to the hotplate and again faced her daughter. "Where did you meet him? How long have you known him?"

Sydney shrugged. "I don't know. He's different from Shawn."

Malcolm laughed. "I don't think there are many people in the world like Shawn."

"Dad!"

"What?"

"There's nothing wrong with Shawn." Sydney glared at her dad, who started to comment, but Victoria nudged him and they shared a quick look. He fell silent.

Victoria crossed the space between her and the island bench to rest her hands on the benchtop. "That sounds fair. You can invite a guest if you're going to make the meal."

"And I can have the car tomorrow?" Sydney held her breath, waiting for their reply. Normally she would have expected no argument. But ever since they'd fought about Shawn, her parents had suddenly introduced a lot more rules into her life.

"Who's going?" Victoria asked. She pulled one of her designs towards her, frowning as she grabbed a pencil from her bag, and made a couple of changes.

"Chelsea and I have been planning this for weeks. It's the first day of the school holidays."

"But who else is going with you?" Victoria continued to alter her design, pausing to chew on the end of her pencil.

"We only planned for the two of us to go. And if you're asking if Shawn is going, he's not. He doesn't get out of bed until after ten," Sydney said.

"And you wonder why we've got a problem with him," Malcolm muttered.

"Mal." Victoria's voice was heavy with warning.

Malcolm shrugged. "I'm just saying."

"As long as you're back by five and have dinner ready by six-thirty." Victoria pushed her design towards Sydney. "What do you think? Would you wear it?"

Sydney stared at the drawing. "Is it a necklace?"

Victoria sighed. "I don't know why I bother to ask."

"Dinner's ready." Malcolm shared the scrambled

eggs between the three plates, each with a piece of toast.

Sydney took her plate. "I'm going to eat in my room." She mentally ran through several excuses until she found one that'd work. "I need to get back to my laptop. I'm in the middle of chatting to Chelsea."

"But you haven't even told us about your trip to the museum. Was there much jewellery on display? Do you think it'd be worth us going along for some design ideas?" Victoria asked.

"I don't know." Using her fingers Sydney popped a piece of egg in her mouth and immediately regretted it when a wave of nausea hit her.

"Oh Sydney. You didn't spend the day talking with Chelsea, did you?" Victoria put her plate on the bench near her designs.

Sydney quickly shook her head. "No. Someone stole a stone statue. We didn't get to see everything."

"Not one of your classmates?" Malcolm asked.

"It was life sized. Almost six foot. Not exactly small enough to put in a schoolbag," Sydney said.

"I wonder if there's something on TV about it." Victoria headed for the lounge room, Malcolm at her side, talking about the increase of crime.

Sydney grinned as she escaped to her room. They always ate early. Her parents would be in bed by seven, as they liked to get up ridiculously early and take a walk before they started their day. They believed it improved their creativity. All Sydney knew was it made dinnertime far too early and she needed a snack before bedtime. The only change to their daily routine was Saturday night when they'd stay up till eight-thirty. She'd hated it when she was younger and she'd had to join her parents and sister on their early morning walks. Now it didn't bother her, most of the time.

She entered her bedroom and frowned at the sight of Corrin's sword leaning against the desk beside him. "Why have you got that out?" She gestured towards it.

Corrin paused the documentary and removed the headphones. "It is my sword."

"Yeah, well leave it in the wardrobe. It's bad enough you're in my room. If my parents found that in here too, they'd really freak." Sydney sat on her bed, her legs curled under her, and took a bite of her food. When Corrin continued to watch her, she pointed to the laptop. "Keep watching it. The more you learn the less questions I'll have to answer." And the less guilt she'd feel about telling him to shut up.

Corrin stared at her a moment longer before he returned to his documentary, his sword still by his side. Sydney considered saying something, but decided to finish her dinner first. Egg didn't taste good when it was cold. Maybe she should have eaten with Corrin when she'd bought him fish and chips while they were out. But it had been too early for her to eat dinner. She'd barely finished her meal when a tap on her door brought her to her feet.

"Yeah?" Sydney grabbed Corrin's sword and pushed him towards the ensuite as she pressed it into his hands. She opened her door and leaned against the doorframe as she waited to see what her mum wanted.

"Make sure you write down the ingredients, you need for dinner, on the grocery list." Victoria looked past Sydney. "Are you finished with your plate?"

Sydney stepped back when her mum stepped forward. She glanced around the room then averted her gaze from the armband Corrin had left on her desk. "Yeah. I'll get it." She hurried to the bed where she'd left her plate hoping, almost praying, her mum wouldn't see the armband. She turned around to see her luck was just as good as it had been that morning.

"Where did you get this?" Victoria ran her fingers over the armband. "The detail is amazing. Frank would love to get his hands on the person who made this. The technique they've used looks authentic." Frank was her boss.

"It belongs to Corrin. I forgot to give it back to him." Sydney tried to take it from her mum, but she brushed Sydney's hands away as she continued to examine it.

"You'll have to ask him who made it." Victoria finally handed the armband back and glanced towards the laptop screen. "Car mechanics? Is that what you're considering doing when you finish year twelve this year?"

Sydney ignored the second question, one she'd heard far too often lately, and focused on the first comment. "You can ask Corrin about the armband when he has dinner with us tomorrow night."

Victoria nodded. "Tell him to bring the designer's details with him. Your father and I would love to talk to them about what techniques they used." She left the room, empty plate in hand.

Chapter Six

Sydney shut her door and leaned against it, eyes closed. She took a deep breath and pushed away. She started to open the ensuite door then thought better of it. She tapped lightly instead. "You can come out now."

Corrin opened the door, his sword in one hand. He took the armband Sydney held out to him without a word.

"Don't leave your stuff lying around my room."

With a nod Corrin returned to the laptop. Sydney watched as he sat down, put the headphones on and continued to watch the documentary. Annoyance made her want to snap at him, demand he not ignore her. She took a deep breath and slowly let it out. Was she crazy? She wanted him to have as little to do with her as possible. She wanted him out of her life. He was just one more obstacle standing between her and Shawn. An obstacle she needed to deal with as quickly as possible. If she was lucky, Chelsea might have an idea.

Sydney dropped onto her bed, putting a hand behind her head as she waited for Chelsea to answer the phone. She smiled at the excited greeting.

"Sydney! How was it? Did you see him? No one even noticed you were gone. Not even when we were getting on the bus to go back to school. You couldn't have picked a better day. The place was crazy. There were cops all over the building and Michelle was doing her drama queen act and hyperventilating and thinking she was next. Why would anyone want to steal her after they'd stolen an ancient stone statue?"

Sydney laughed. She could clearly picture Michelle's dramatics. "Typical. She was probably annoyed she wasn't the centre of attention."

"Yeah, but forget that. How was Shawn?"

"Annoyed. I didn't make it."

"What happened? And please start from the very beginning. Like when I left you behind the statue? Oh no! You weren't there when they stole him, were you?"

Sydney took a deep breath and told Chelsea everything that had happened. There was silence on the other end of the phone when she'd finished. "Are you still there, Chelz?"

"Sydney." Chelsea's voice was hesitant. "Do you want me to come over? Are you alright?"

"You don't believe me, do you?"

"It's not that I don't believe you. It's just that…" her voice trailed off.

Sydney watched as Corrin put the headphones aside and stood up, stretching. His shirt rose, exposing several centimetres of skin and some scars on his back. She looked away. "I'll meet you at the park. I'll bring him with me. Then you'll see." The park was across the road from Chelsea's house.

"You can't come all that way at night on your own," Chelsea said.

"I won't be on my own."

"But-"

"I'll see you there soon." Sydney disconnected, annoyed her best friend now thought she was losing her mind. She turned towards Corrin. "We're going out." Her gaze dropped to his hand that reached for his sword. "And you're not taking that. Put it in my wardrobe. What is it? Your security blanket?"

"What-" Oh forget it. Just hurry up." Sydney headed for the floor length curtain and drew it aside to unlock a glass sliding door. It was a pity this door could only be locked from the inside. It'd make things a lot easier if she could use this as her entrance, but her parents had refused to put an external lock on it.

She stepped onto the paved area outside her room and thought for about the hundredth time that she really needed to buy a couple of chairs for the area. Although with the amount of money she'd spent on Corrin today she'd be surprised if she had enough left in her account to buy anything.

"Where are we going?" Corrin watched as she slid the door shut. "And do not tell me forget it. I did not ask to be bound to you. You throw around more orders than a chieftain does."

"We're going to meet my best friend. Now quiet. I don't want my parents to hear us. They'd freak if they knew I was sneaking out."

"And I guess you are not going to explain this freak to me either."

"Shh."

Sydney hurried down the street, glaring at the couple of dogs that raced at their fences to bark at them. Ten minutes later they arrived at the park where Chelsea sat on a swing that she spun from side to side. As soon as she spotted them, she was on her feet.

Chelsea gestured towards Corrin. "Who's he? What happened today? Where did you meet him?"

Sydney ignored most of the questions. "Corrin, this is Chelsea."

"I am allowed to talk now?" Corrin asked.

"Not if you're going to ask me more questions. I swear you're going to drive me insane," Sydney said.

"I need to understand your world. Knowledge is as important as strength in a battle," Corrin said.

"He speaks strange." Chelsea stared at Corrin.

Sydney dropped onto one of the pair of swings near them, stepping out of the light cast from the streetlamp. "What did you expect? That's probably how they spoke in the Dark Ages."

Chelsea sat in the other swing. "You're not going to stick to that story, are you?"

Sydney leapt to her feet. "When have I ever lied to you?"

"Yeah, but I mean, come on Sydney. You can't really expect me to believe that." Chelsea looked around. "There's a film crew waiting somewhere, isn't there. It's one of those shows like Pranked or something. They're cruel, Sydney. I thought better of you than that."

Sydney grabbed a couple of tissues out of the back pocket of her jeans. She handed one to Corrin and pointed to the far side of the park. "Walk that way until your nose bleeds, then come back."

Corrin stared at her a moment before he nodded. "If you need me before then call for me. Who knows what is hiding in the shadows."

"We'll be okay. Now hurry up."

Corrin smiled. "You use that okay word all the time." He turned and walked away before Sydney could comment.

With a last glare at his back, she stepped into the light cast by the street lamp and faced Chelsea. "Watch me. Tell me what you see."

"You're worrying me, Sydney. You're not on drugs are you? Shawn didn't give you something, did he?"

"What is it with people and questions lately?" Sydney forced herself to stay still when she wanted to run after Corrin. Already her skin felt far too small to cover her bones and nausea was starting to rise. Maybe she shouldn't have had dinner. Then her nose started to run and the sharp metallic scent of blood filled the air around her. She brought the tissue up and pressed it against her nose, her gaze holding Chelsea's.

Chelsea stared at Sydney, mouth open and a hand stretched out as if afraid to touch her, but wanting desperately to help her friend. "Sydney." The word was a whisper. "You went white. As white as Shawn. I didn't think you could go white. It's not your natural skin colour."

"White?" Last time she'd only paled slightly.

Chelsea nodded her head. "Like all your skin was slowly bleached of colour." Her hand was still outstretched. "What happened to you?"

"I didn't lie. Not to you, Chelz. Never to you."

"Oh my god." Chelsea pulled back her outstretched hand to press it to her mouth. "You stole the statue."

"Shh. And I didn't steal him. He walked out of there on his own." Sydney looked over Chelsea's shoulder as Corrin rejoined them.

Chelsea looked behind her and gave a squeak before she scurried to Sydney's side. "What are you going to do with him, Sydney? You can't keep him. What would your parents say?"

"They can't find out. They wouldn't believe me." Sydney grabbed Chelsea by the shoulders. "Do you understand, Chelz? They can't find out."

"But this is serious. It's not like sneaking out for a few hours at night. Or even ditching school to meet up with your boyfriend."

"Which I didn't manage to do thanks to Corrin," Sydney pointed out.

"He could murder you in your sleep," Chelsea's voice rose a notch.

Sydney shook her friend's shoulders slightly. "Stop it, Chelz. You're getting hysterical."

Corrin stepped closer. "I would never kill Sydney. It would be suicide."

Sydney's hands fell to her side as she turned to Corrin. "What?"

"I would never–" Corrin started to say.

"No. I heard you. I want to know what it means," Sydney said.

"We are bound."

Sydney felt her patience shred even further. She spoke through clenched teeth. "And what exactly does that mean?"

"Why is it fine for you to ask questions and yet I am not allowed?" Corrin asked mildly.

Sydney stabbed a finger at his chest. "Answer right now before I am the one doing murder. What does being bound mean exactly? And make the explanation four-year-old simple."

"If you die so do I."

Sydney stared at Corrin, her finger still at his chest. "And if you die?"

Corrin did not answer immediately. His gaze continued to hold Sydney's. "So do you."

Neither of them took notice of Chelsea's gasp and sudden step backwards.

Sydney balled her fist and swung it at Corrin who grabbed it in midair, holding it tight. "Damn you! Fix this. I don't want to be bound. Deal with it right now. Do you hear me?" She tried to pull away from him.

Corrin continued to hold her fist. "Then set me a great service to perform for you."

"I have no idea what a great service is. No one even talks like that anymore. So what happens if there's no great service?"

"We are bound forever."

"I am so screwed." Sydney tugged on her hand and this time Corrin let her go. She turned away from him, uncertain where to go. "Absolutely screwed," she muttered.

Chapter Seven

Chelsea took a step towards Sydney, hand reaching out as if to comfort. Before she managed to touch Sydney's shoulder, her hand dropped away. "You'll figure it out. You're the master of plans."

"Yeah, right." Sydney laughed sharply. "And how many of them work?"

Chelsea's hand rose again then once more fell to her side. "Nearly half your plans work. Besides, I'll help you."

Sydney swore. "How? You can't even touch me. What are you afraid of? That I'm contagious?"

"Are you?" Chelsea looked from Sydney to Corrin.

"The binding is done. There is only one way to change it," Corrin said.

Sydney strode back to the swings and dropped onto one. Her throat ached, her eyes burned. How had everything gone so crazy so quickly? "What the hell am I meant to do now? It was an effort to stay in the kitchen with my parents tonight. Chelsea, you know how little distance there is between the kitchen and my room. What the hell am I meant to do? And what about when school starts again in a fortnight? What then?"

Chelsea sat in the swing beside her. "I don't know." Her voice sounded small and far away.

Sydney watched as Corrin ran his hands up the metal posts that curved out of the ground to support the chains of the swings. He turned his gaze to the chains. Guilt hit her again. She guessed all this mess wasn't Corrin's fault. He wasn't the first male to be taken in by a viper. She tried to think of the woman's name, but only the word viper had stuck. Probably because it was the name that suited her the most. "It's a swing."

Corrin reached out to touch the chain of the swing Sydney sat on. "What is the purpose of the swing?"

"Fun."

"Fun?"

Sydney nodded and rose to her feet. This was something she could explain. Something she understood. "Sit down."

"And stay?" Corrin sat on the seat she'd vacated.

Sydney laughed. "Yeah. I wouldn't suggest getting

off right now." She walked behind him. "Hold onto the chain and don't let go." She tugged on the chain, barely pulling the swing back at all. As he again swung towards her, she pressed both her hands against his back and pushed him forward. She kept at it until the momentum increased. Beside him, Chelsea had her own swing going faster, her legs pumping back and forth.

"You need to move your legs. Watch me," Chelsea called out to Corrin.

After watching Chelsea a moment, Corrin mimicked her and as he learned the rhythm, he swung higher. His laughter filled the air. "And this is what you do for fun in your world? Does no one celebrate with food and drink?"

Sydney laughed. "Yeah. Amongst other things. But this is fun for little kids. Or so people keep telling me. It doesn't matter though. I still like it, no matter what anyone says. Lean back and look at the stars with your legs stretched out in front of you."

Chelsea did as Sydney suggested before she called out, "Like this Corrin."

Sydney watched them. Her best friend on a swing next to an ancient warrior. He looked far too young to have been born centuries ago. "How old are you, Corrin?"

Corrin sat back up. "I thought on that question. I was given my first real blade when I was five. Four years later I was sent to be fostered with our chieftain. The following year Lorcan became my blood brother and then it was two years before we were in our first battle. Three years after that, Lorcan met Orlaith. It took him two years to convince her to marry him. She wanted him to prove his love for her in battles and plunder. We earned a fortune from raids and battles. And she was only with him a year before she ran away and I failed my brother."

Sydney kept count on her fingers as he spoke. "You're eighteen? You're only a year older than me?" She couldn't help staring at him. "Seriously?"

Corrin shrugged. "I guess."

"You can't count?" Sydney continued to stare at him as the swing slowed.

"I can count enough. I know more important things. I always win at contests of strength, skill and hunting. My father was skilled in metal work so I have some knowledge of his craft. I do not understand your obsession with the knowledge of writing and counting. Even the druids know that to write things down takes their magic from them. How can you still have so much magic in your world with this obsession of writing?"

"That's how our world runs. With the knowledge of writing and counting. And there is no magic. It's technology," Sydney said.

Chelsea's swing slowed to a stop. "You mean he's illiterate?"

"Will everyone please stop sidetracking me?"

Chelsea laughed. "You don't need our help for that."

Sydney made a face at Chelsea. "Why are we best friends?"

Chelsea's smile stayed in place. "Because I'm the only one stupid enough to think you might not be completely crazy."

"Thanks. Your confidence in me is overwhelming." Sydney turned to Corrin. "Can I have the swing back? Some of my best plans were made on a swing."

"Not to mention some of your worst," Chelsea said.

Sydney gestured towards Chelsea with her middle finger as she got comfortable on the swing. "What we really need is to get away for a week or two. We need some space to think this over and sort out what to do. Somewhere I can stay near Corrin. It's too painful being far apart. Not to mention the nosebleeds are disgusting." She looked over her shoulder when Corrin grabbed hold of the chains and pulled the swing towards him. Within moments she was swinging higher, her legs pumping back and forth. The wind rushed against her face and she flung her head back to watch the stars spin out of control. Her lips reluctantly formed a smile. There was no way she could be annoyed when she was on a swing. It was like being free. No cares, only her and the wind rushing by.

"I've got it." Chelsea jumped off her swing in mid motion, landing on her feet. "I've got it."

Sydney waited until her swing had slowed enough before she did the same, bending her knees to take the impact. "What?"

"My grandma's house."

Sydney stared at Chelsea, still confused. "But she's not there."

"Exactly. Her things need to be packed up and no one wants to do it."

Sydney started to smile. "But if you seem too eager, they'll wonder what we're up to."

"Not if we wait until after we go to the beach tomorrow. We can both complain about how far it is and how much time we'd planned to spend there these holidays. It's spring. Who wouldn't want to live at the beach in spring? If we stay at Grandma's house we can be at the beach within fifteen minutes. And we'll have the middle of the day and evenings to pack up the house."

Sydney grabbed hold of Chelsea's hands and spun around with her. "We're brilliant!"

"Of course we are." Chelsea fell against Sydney in a fit of laughter.

"That is one thing that is the same as my world."

They turned to look at Corrin, arms around each other's waists. It was Sydney who asked the question both wanted answered. "What's the same?"

"Girls are still impossible to understand."

Sydney and Chelsea looked at each other and burst into laughter again. When they finally stopped, Sydney said, "I'll pick you up around nine-thirty. My parents have to get groceries in the morning."

"So much for an entire day at the beach." Chelsea fell quiet for a moment. "Sorry I freaked before. But, you know."

"Yeah. It's a bit much to get your head around, isn't it?"

"Are you okay?" Chelsea rested her hand on Sydney's shoulder, staring intently at her. "Seriously?"

Sydney nodded. "I will be. We're going to sort this out." She grinned. "Aren't I the master of plans?"

Chelsea grinned back at her. "Of course you are."

"Text me when you get home."

Chelsea nodded then headed for her house. Sydney watched her friend walk away for a moment before she glanced towards Corrin and headed for her own home. He fell into step beside her, his head turning at each sound.

"What are you looking for?" Sydney asked.

"Danger. You should have let me bring my sword."

"That wouldn't help with most of the dangers you'd find in my world. Could your sword stop a bullet?"

"How can I answer that when I do not know what one is?"

Sydney sighed. She should have known better than to start a discussion with Corrin. It always led to questions.

"Let me guess. Forget it?"

Sydney grinned as she glanced at him. "Yeah."

They walked the rest of the way home in silence. Not even the sound of the phone beeping, when Chelsea's text came through, brought a question from Corrin. The silence lasted through Sydney throwing a couple of blankets and a pillow on the floor for Corrin and each of them using the bathroom. Before getting into bed, Sydney hurried to the kitchen to scribble a few items on the grocery list, running back to her room as she fought against throwing up.

Locking the door, she crawled into bed, a snack the furthest thing from her mind.

"Goodnight, Corrin."

There was another moment of silence before Corrin spoke. "I will help you with your plan, Sydney of Brisbane."

"It's Sydney Cooper. People have first and last names here. Do you have last names in your time?"

"We are known by where we are from, who we are related to or by what we have achieved."

"And what are you known by?"

"After I left childhood I was known as Corrin brother of Lorcan. We were always together. Mostly now I am known as Corrin Harbinger of Death."

"What is a harbinger?"

"The one sent ahead to warn of who or what is coming."

"Why were you warning people death was coming?"

"How else could I help Lorcan win Orlaith? I lost count of the battles I won for him. First by his side then alone as he stayed to protect the wealth we had gained."

Sydney thought of all the scars on Corrin's body. Had he gained anything from putting his life at risk to help his brother win a viper? She couldn't bring herself to ask. What sort of person would put their own life at risk to help another win their dream? Then turn around and believe the lies someone told about that person. Either the viper had been very convincing or there was something Corrin wasn't telling her. Maybe he had wanted the viper for himself.

She fell into a dream filled sleep. A woman, with vipers twined around her, draped herself over Corrin. Laughing, she dragged him away from Sydney. Sydney tried to grab hold of him but he pushed her away. The woman took Corrin further and further away as Sydney's body shrunk in on itself until only dust remained to blow away in the breeze.

Chapter Eight

Morning had Sydney fighting her sheets as she struggled to sit up, gasping for breath. She felt whole, her skin normal. She stared down at her light brown hands. Colour normal. She tried to slow her breathing. It had only been a dream.

"Sydney?"

She looked over to where Corrin stood in the doorway of the ensuite. He wore a pair of jeans, his hair damp and loose around his shoulders. "I'm okay."

Corrin continued to stare at her for a moment before he nodded. "Is there somewhere I can train?"

"Train?" A frown creased her brow.

"With my sword."

Sydney shook her head. "No. At least I don't think so." She glanced at her alarm clock. It was just after eight. "It depends if my parents are home. But then, I don't know how long they'll be gone either." She slumped back against her pillow. "Always questions. Can't you at least wait until I'm awake?"

"Your eyes are open and you are talking. Does that not mean awake in this time?"

With a glare, Sydney threw her pillow at him and muttered when he caught it. She rolled over onto her stomach. "Just great. I'd have to be stuck with someone who loves mornings. I might as well go drown myself."

Corrin sat on the bed beside her. "That sounds a little drastic. Especially since I do not love mornings. I wake immediately I open my eyes, day or night. Life is safer that way."

Sydney turned on her side and put her arm under her head. "You take everything so literally. It was just, oh I don't know. It was an expression of annoyance I guess. I don't like to wake up. And I'm worse in winter. Even if I've had ten hours sleep. I'd rather laze in my bed just a little longer because I'm comfortable. Or in winter because I'm warm."

"Can we break our fast?"

"Breakfast?"

Corrin shrugged. "I am hungry."

Sydney sat up. "You know I think I've figured out part of why you sound so strange. You don't use contractions. You say I am. While I say I'm."

"I'm hungry."

Sydney chuckled as she threw the sheets back. "Okay. Let me use the bathroom and see if my parents are home."

"They have already left. Their noise woke me."

Sydney nodded. "I'll be a minute." She grabbed her bikini and a sundress and headed for her ensuite. When she came out fifteen minutes later she laughed at the sight of Corrin on her bed, leaned up against her bed head flicking through one of her magazines. "The clothes in that one are so last season, do you want me to buy you a new one while we're out?"

Corrin put the magazine on the bed as he rose. "You will have to explain your jest. I am… I'm afraid I do not understand it."

Sydney shook her head. Before she could answer, Corrin beat her to it.

"I know. Forget it."

"Okay. I'm sorry. I'll answer some of your questions. But please, don't ask so many." She headed for her bedroom door then paused to look back at Corrin. "Are you sure they're gone?"

"We are alone in your place."

Sydney met his gaze, her hand on the doorknob. Alone. She pushed the word from her mind and forced herself to turn back to the door and open it, striding to the kitchen. Alone. How many times had she wanted that word to be about her and Shawn? His place had always seemed to be full of people during the month she'd been seeing him. And she couldn't bring him here. Her parents would freak. And it wasn't fair because they hadn't given him a chance. Ten minutes with him and they'd hated him. How could you form an opinion of a person that quickly?

"Is something wrong?"

"No. Nothing." Sydney swung open the door of the fridge. "What do you normally eat for breakfast?" She felt Corrin's warmth behind her as he peered into the fridge.

"What is all of this?"

His breath brushed across her cheek but there was no space to step away. "Food."

"Food?"

She turned enough to press her hand against his chest. "Give me some space. And where is your shirt? Do you normally go around half naked?"

"Yes. Now how is this food? You said you would answer some of my questions."

"Milk, apricot cheese, bread, jam, honey, butter, lettuce, tomatoes, corn, whipped cream, chocolate, tinned fruit, sauces, mayonnaise and a tonne of eggs." Sydney pointed to each in turn.

"All this is edible?"

"Yes. Well, kind of. You can eat all of it, but some of it goes with stuff. Like the sauces. You wouldn't eat them on their own. They're to add flavour to things. Like on a burger. Or meat."

"You do eat meat? I do not see any in here."

"It's in the freezer."

Corrin reached out and gently pressed the half loaf of bread. "This is bread?"

"What does your bread look like?"

"Flat." The fridge started to beep and Corrin jumped back, pulling Sydney with him.

"It's okay. It's just the fridge letting me know I've left the door open too long." She pushed the door shut. "See. It's quiet now."

"It talks to you?" Corrin eyed it warily.

"Ah, not exactly. Look, you go and put on a shirt and I'll make breakfast. You don't have any objection to bacon, do you? Pig?"

"You keep pigs?"

Sydney shook her head. "No more questions until after breakfast. Now go get a shirt on." She felt her skin tighten as he left the room and hurriedly got eggs, tomatoes, bread and butter from the fridge and bacon from the freezer. While bacon thawed in the microwave she took out a frypan.

By the time Corrin returned, Sydney was flipping eggs and buttering toast. She gestured towards the island bench and the stools on the far side of it. "Sit."

"And stay?"

Sydney made a face at him. "Watch it or I won't feed you." She flipped the eggs onto the plates that already had two pieces of toast. Bacon and fried tomatoes followed. Grabbing cutlery, she took the plates with her to the bench where she'd already placed two glasses of water.

"What is this?" Corrin looked through the loose pages of designs Victoria had left on the benchtop.

"Mum's work." Sydney took a mouthful of water.

"That is safe?" Corrin pointed to the glass. At Sydney's nod, he took a cautious sip. "You have a spring?"

Sydney grinned. "Not exactly. It's bottled water. Mum buys it because she thinks town water tastes revolting. It says on the label it comes from a spring. And what happened to no questions until after breakfast?"

Corrin shrugged as he looked over the designs again. "She is trying to use my arm band as her inspiration. It is destroying the meaning behind it."

"Meaning?"

"The story. Everything has a story. This line, it is no good. She should continue with this part of the-"

Sydney held her hand up. "You're talking to the artistically challenged." She picked up a blank piece of paper and a pencil. "Here. Knock yourself out."

Corrin frowned. "You want me to do what?"

"Draw your idea. No point explaining it to me. Besides, my breakfast is getting cold." She picked up her cutlery and, cutting off a piece of her food, ate it.

Corrin placed the paper and pencil beside his plate and eyed the fork he picked up. "This is meant to be better than fingers?"

Sydney shrugged. "Cleaner anyway."

Corrin watched her a moment longer then tried to mimic how she used her cutlery. It took him a couple of attempts before he understood the principle. He swallowed the mouthful he managed to get to his mouth with the fork, and grinned. "A clever idea." He nodded towards the fork.

Sydney returned his grin. "Sometimes. Not when it comes to pizza though."

"Pizza?"

Sydney shook her head and started to speak when Corrin laughed. Her eyes narrowed. "Watch it," she warned. She saw the question in his expression, but still smiling he turned back to his food instead of asking it. She watched as he picked up the pencil and tested it on the paper. His strokes became bolder as he sketched his own ideas in between mouthfuls.

Drawing and meal finished, Corrin pushed the paper towards Sydney. "Does that not look much better?"

Sydney shrugged. "I don't know. I need things in 3D. Mum has just about given up on asking my opinion on any of her drawings. Sometimes she asks, but I think it's more out of hope than expecting anything of me."

"3D?"

Sydney held up her fork. "This is 3D. Three dimensional. If you draw a picture of it, it would be 2D. I need the object to be able to give you an opinion. Or a real picture of it. But there has to be something in it for size comparison. And not a ruler. Like a person or something. But then that can be difficult because you don't know if the person is tall or short."

"Will you be annoyed if I have to ask several questions before I can make proper sense out of what you said?"

"Probably." Sydney froze at the sound of the front door opening. She swore. It was too late. There was no way she could explain two breakfast plates. At least Corrin wasn't half naked. She pasted on a smile and rose to her feet, noticing Corrin did the same. "Morning Mum, Dad."

Chapter Nine

Victoria stopped partway into the kitchen, several grocery bags in her hands. "Who is this?"

"Corrin. He dropped in to pick up his armband and I was just starting breakfast. Corrin, this is my mum, Victoria and my dad, Mal." Sydney gestured first towards her mum and then her dad who stood behind Victoria.

Corrin stepped forward. "Can I help you with your bags?"

Mal smiled. "There's more in the car. That's an offer I won't turn down."

Relieved, Sydney grabbed hold of Corrin's wrist and tugged him towards the front door. "Come on before they find something else for us to do. You know you didn't have to offer."

"It is the least I can do in gratitude for the meal,"

Corrin said as they stepped outside. He eyed the car. "This is a motor vehicle?"

"Yeah. A car."

He walked around the outside of the compact white hatchback. He peered into the open back door to the bags of groceries spread out on the seat. "It does not have much space. They seemed bigger in your documentary."

Sydney grabbed a couple of bags. "They come in different sizes."

"Could your family not afford a larger car?"

"Yeah, but it's easier to park this in the city."

Corrin took the last of the bags, gathering six in one hand and seven in the other. "A horse would take up less space."

Sydney bumped the door shut with her hip. "But they take more effort to look after. Besides, cars go faster than horses." She led the way inside, kicking the front door closed behind them, heading for the kitchen. She stopped suddenly when she noticed her parents holding Corrin's design.

"Who did this?" Victoria held up the piece of paper.

"I did." Corrin stepped forward and put the groceries on the bench near the rest of them. "You had the story wrong."

"Story?" Victoria looked from the drawing to Corrin. "Did you make your armband?"

Corrin shook his head. "My father made it. He enjoyed working with metals."

Victoria put the piece of paper down next to her own designs. "We'd love to meet him."

"That is not possible. He is dead."

"I'm sorry. Was he a jeweller? He was very talented."

"No, a warrior."

"Soldier," Sydney quickly corrected.

"Was he killed in the line of duty?" Victoria asked.

Sydney answered before Corrin had a chance. "Yes."

"And your mother?" Victoria asked.

"He has no family," Sydney said when she saw Corrin about to speak again.

"Let the poor boy speak, Sydney," Malcolm said. "We want to hear more about his father. Where did he train?"

"His own father taught him. My father would have preferred to be only a… jeweller, but," Corrin frowned and looked towards Sydney.

"He had to support his family," Sydney said. "He didn't make enough money being a jeweller."

"What a waste of talent," Victoria said. "Did he

teach you?" She gestured towards the drawing Corrin had made.

Corrin shrugged. "A little."

Victoria held out the design she'd shown Sydney the previous night. "Maybe you could have a look at this and tell me what you think."

"Mum! I'm going to the beach. We don't have time for this."

"I thought you said only you and Chelsea are going," Victoria said.

"We are, but I said I'd drop Corrin off on the way. He'll be here for dinner. You can ask him then." Sydney tried to pull Corrin from the kitchen.

Corrin gently shrugged her off. "I will only be a moment."

"Fine," Sydney muttered. "I'll get my gear." She stalked from the kitchen and ignored the tightening of her skin. She grabbed a couple of towels, underwear, Corrin's board shorts and sunscreen. She shoved everything in her beach bag and headed back to the kitchen. She stared at her parents and Corrin who were busy arguing the merits of different metals and what would showcase the bracelet best. Sydney shook her head. And she'd thought it was a necklace. She grabbed two bottles of water from the cupboard and some snack food before she turned back to

Corrin, hands on her hips. "A moment expired minutes ago."

Corrin looked up as if surprised to see her there. He smiled and rubbed at his arm, causing the long sleeve of his shirt to rise and reveal more scars. "I'm sorry. We can go now."

"How did you get all those scars?" Victoria stared at his arm.

Sydney quickly answered. "Car accident."

"That's dreadful." Victoria reached out and pulled the sleeve back further. "Surely they could have used cosmetic surgery to minimise these."

"Mum! Please! Leave him alone. How would you like to be poked and prodded like some oddity?"

"I didn't." Victoria turned to Corrin. "You didn't mind me asking, did you?"

Sydney crossed the kitchen and grabbed Corrin by the wrist. "Let's go before she decides to adopt you. An orphan with a talent for jewellery. Just don't tell her you can cook or she'll never let you go."

Victoria laughed. "You exaggerate, Sydney." She paused and looked over to Corrin. "Can you cook?"

Malcolm dropped an arm around Victoria's shoulders. "Make sure you're back by five, Sydney."

"Okay, bye." Sydney grabbed the car keys and, with her hand still wrapped around Corrin's wrist, headed for the front door. She let him go as soon as they were outside. "They weren't too traumatic, were they?"

"I like your parents. Your mother is a little intense sometimes, but nice all the same." Corrin slid into the car seat, looking crowded.

Sydney showed him how to slide the seat back. "Just be careful what you tell them. They don't need to know you're from the Dark Ages."

Corrin nodded. "I know. You were very clear on that last night."

Sydney stood by his open door and stared down at him a moment longer. What was it about Corrin that her parents preferred over Shawn? He was gorgeous, but then so was Shawn in her opinion. Was it just because Corrin had talked jewellery with them? Or was it because Shawn was her boyfriend and Corrin wasn't? Maybe they didn't really want her to date even though they said she could. None of her questions seemed to have answers. She felt a moment of sympathy for Corrin as she closed his door, ignoring his questioning look. You and me both, she thought. There are a million questions and none of them have any answers.

Chapter Ten

Sydney smiled as she listened to Chelsea and Corrin, who both sat in the back seat. Chelsea had spent the day playing teacher. Her smile faded as she recalled seeing the scars that criss-crossed Corrin's body. Lucky her mum hadn't seen all of them or she'd have been booking him in for cosmetic surgery.

"Don't. Not do not," Chelsea said.

"I don't see why it is so important to talk like you do," Corrin said.

"Why it's," Chelsea corrected.

"Do I need to learn every single contraction in one day?"

Chelsea turned towards Sydney. "You know what I think he needs? A week long movie marathon. That'd have him talking right in no time."

Sydney pulled up in front of Chelsea's house. "We can take a stack to your grandma's house. But no gangsta movies. We don't want him talking like that."

"Sounds like a plan." Chelsea grinned. "A master plan."

Sydney laughed. "Just make sure you con your parents into letting us stay there."

"You've got nothing to worry about. You taught me everything I know about conning parents." Chelsea opened the car door then stopped to pull a DVD out of her bag and hand it to Corrin.

He took the item and turned it back and forth. "What is this?"

"Alphabet. It's aimed at little kids, but if it works, who cares?"

"Little kids? Like swings?"

Chelsea laughed. "Not quite." She looked over to Sydney. "I'll call you later. After I've done my 'this drive is killing me' routine." She clambered out of the car, and with a wave, headed towards her front door.

Corrin got in the front of the car, still turning the DVD over. "What is this for?"

"You can watch it on my laptop. Like the documentary, but it's about letters instead of cars."

"I have lived my entire life without letters. I don't need them now."

"But you lived in the Dark Ages. This time is

different. You can't just settle problems with fighting."

"You told me soldiers are like warriors."

"Like. Not the same. But even soldiers need to be able to read. It's not all about killing."

"Killing is all I have a talent for."

Sydney shook her head. "No. No one has only that for a talent. You're more than Corrin Harbinger of Death. Much more."

Corrin smiled. "You make it sound like that is a terrible name. It's a name to be proud of. Not everyone could earn such a name."

Sydney didn't know how to reply to his comment. How could he not be bothered by that name? "You killed people to be able to get your name."

"Only the enemy. But it's not only that. It also means I was not the one who died. I lived. I won."

Sydney pulled up in her driveway and faced Corrin. "And that's what's important? Winning?"

"No. Winning with honour is important."

The front door burst open before Sydney could think what to say and Victoria hurried over to the car, opening Corrin's door. "About time you pair arrived. I want you to look at the design and tell me what you think of it now. And I'd love to have a closer look at your torc." She gestured towards the metal around his neck.

"I never take it off." Corrin climbed out of the car.

"They used to indicate a man's standing in the world. One like yours would have been worn by a very important man. A great warrior. Maybe even a king," Victoria said.

"I know."

Sydney followed behind Corrin and her mum. A king? Had he been a king in his own time? And now what was he? An illiterate teenager who was bound to a girl who kept telling him to shut up. Why hadn't he said anything? Sydney threw her beach bag inside her room as she passed it. She'd unpack it later. Why hadn't he said how important he was? And why did he listen when she told him to shut up? She thought back to their conversation in the alley.

She pictured Corrin standing proudly, his hand on the hilt of his sword as he spoke. "You are more than my chieftain while we are bound. Anything you ask of me, if it is in my power to do so, I will."

Did that mean he had no choice other than to follow her orders? How would it feel going from Harbinger of Death to being ordered around by a teenager whose only claim to fame was that she had a tendency to make grand plans? And grand didn't necessarily mean they worked.

Sydney's slow steps finally brought her to the empty kitchen and she guessed everyone had just retreated to her parent's workroom. Which was probably why her skin felt ten sizes too small and her head ached. Not to mention her bones felt like they were being ground together and she struggled not to throw up. If her nose started to bleed she was dragging him to the kitchen to help. And she didn't care if he was having too much fun showing her parents what they'd failed to produce in their two attempts at having kids. She swung the fridge door open too fast and grabbed it when it started to close again. Staring at the contents, she tried to recall what she'd planned to cook.

Her headache eased and the rest of her symptoms reduced until they were gone. She turned around and saw Corrin several steps away. "What?"

"Feel better now?"

Sydney rubbed her temples. "Yeah."

"I could not think of a way to decline. I'm sorry. I did not mean to cause you so much pain." He reached out and rubbed her temples, his fingers warm against her skin.

Sydney let the fridge door go and heard it close

as she shut her eyes. "Your fingers are magic. My headache is nearly gone." She swayed towards him.

"You are right. We need somewhere to plan. Somewhere we can be together."

Sydney's eyes flew open at his words and she stepped away from him. "You're only hanging around until we're no longer bound. And don't forget that tomorrow we need to visit my boyfriend. Tomorrow you're Chelsea's friend. Don't you dare forget."

Corrin only nodded and turned away from her. "I don't know how you cook in your time, but in my own time I cooked many a meal if you need help."

Sydney was tempted to remake her point but decided it might be best to let Corrin change the subject. "What did you use for cooking? I'm guessing you didn't have an oven." A gust of wind outside had her reaching for the window over the sink to close it.

"I cooked over an open fire."

"I haven't had food cooked on a fire since I was a little kid. Mum and Dad took us camping a few times. Mum didn't really like it. She's more of a resort kind of person." The window shook again and Sydney paused to look outside. Maybe a storm was on the way. Hopefully not. She hated to drive in pouring rain. Returning to the fridge, she started to take food out and place it on the bench. "Maybe we better keep you on simple things for now. A stove might be too much for a beginner to start with. How does cutting up salad sound?" She pulled a sharp knife from the block on the bench and held it out, handle first, to Corrin.

He grinned at her. "A blade. I've got a talent for blades."

Sydney rolled her eyes. "I'm beginning to think you've got a talent for BS."

"And I guess you're not going to explain what BS is?"

"Nope. But it's something you and a bull have in common." Sydney didn't let herself smile until she had her back to Corrin. Her smile became a grin when she heard him laugh.

"Hmm. I guess I'll just have to prove myself. What do you want me to attack first?"

Sydney grabbed several tomatoes from the bench and threw them to Corrin. She was surprised he caught each of them without effort. "Wash them at the sink first then slice them." She watched him for a moment and deciding he was doing fine, she focused on cooking up the steaks she'd requested on the shopping list.

Dinner was ready on time and Adelaide breezed in

with minutes to spare, Evan following in her wake. Luckily Adelaide monopolised the conversation and there were no more awkward questions for Corrin to sidestep. When dinner was finished Sydney pretended to see him off at the front door then dashed into her room to let him in her sliding door. She returned to the kitchen to spend a few more minutes with her family. It was one of the few times she was glad her parents liked early nights. It meant she could escape to her room and let her skin go back to its normal size.

Corrin was at her laptop watching the DVD when she entered. She had set it up when she'd let him in. When she continued to stand near him, he paused the program and removed the headphones. "Is something wrong?"

"I don't know, you tell me. When we're apart and my body feels like it wants to implode, is that causing me any long term harm? Like I don't know, an aneurysm or something."

"How am I expected to answer? Your words leave me with unanswered questions that make it impossible for me to understand what you have said."

"Will it kill me if we're apart too long?"

"Yes."

Sydney's mouth opened. Not a single word came

out. She tried again. "It's killing me? Every time we're apart?"

"Not exactly. Those are warning signs. If you ignore them, the signs become worse until you cannot heal."

"I don't want to die." Sydney reached for her desk, feeling light headed.

Corrin stood. He put an arm around her waist and guided her to the bed. "You will not die. Not until you are old. Sit. Before you fall." He sat beside her on the bed. "Everything will be," he paused and smiled. "Okay?"

Sydney's answering smile was weak. "You promise I won't die?"

"I promise to do everything in my power to keep you alive." Corrin draped his arm around her shoulders. "I don't plan to die and since we are bound that means I need you alive for my own existence."

She rested her head against his chest and thought of her dream where she turned to dust. "What does Orlaith look like?"

Corrin didn't answer immediately. "Not quite your height. Slimmer. Delicate looking. Large blue eyes and reddish brown hair. Skin like a pale honey." He laughed softly. "She wasn't the woman she looked. I saw her put an arrow through a man after kneeing him for touching her. He lay on the ground at her feet and before he could even make a sound at the pain, there was an arrow through his heart. She was a great hunter. She could take anything down with her bow."

"Did you love her?"

"Like a sister. Lorcan was my brother so she became my sister. When she asked for my protection I felt honour bound to give it. It would have been better had she put an arrow through my heart."

"No!" She pulled away to look up at him and shook her head. "No."

Corrin smiled slightly. "Then you would not be sitting here worried about your aneurysm."

"You don't even know what it is."

"No, but I'm sure it is very bad with how you freak."

"Are freaked out," Sydney automatically corrected.

"Are you now okay?"

She pulled further away with a nod of her head. "Yeah."

"Then I'll go back to the little kid documentary." Corrin rose to his feet.

"Little kid show or little kid DVD." Sydney smiled. A sudden gust at the sliding door caught her attention and she eyed the closed curtain. "I hope it doesn't storm."

"No. It does not smell like rain."

Sydney stared at him as he returned to the laptop. Laying back on her bed, she picked up her phone. There were no missed calls. What was taking Chelsea so long? She debated ringing her, but didn't want to ruin any plan with wrong timing. Dropping her phone on the bed, she rose to her feet and strode across the room to step outside. She left the sliding door open and the wind whipped around her, making the curtain flick about. She breathed deep. Corrin was right. She couldn't smell rain in the air. But that didn't mean it wasn't coming. She turned to go inside and the movement of a shadow drew her attention. A hibiscus against the fence shuddered in the wind and Sydney shrugged, guessing it had been the plant that had caught her attention.

Once again she started to go inside when the wind pushed against her, looking almost like a woman, long hair whipping around her as she shoved at Sydney. Fear and anger bloomed in her and she struck out at the whirling image that became clearer. She struggled to enter her room as the wind buffeted her.

Chapter Eleven

Corrin was on his feet and by her side in seconds, dragging her inside and sliding the door shut. He grabbed Sydney by the shoulders. "You are unhurt?"

Sydney could only nod.

He ran his hands down her arms. "You are certain." One hand went to her chin and tilted her head back. "She did not hurt you?"

"What's happening?"

His fingers left her chin to rest on her chest just below her pulse point. "I need to make you an amulet. You must never take it off. Gold. It needs to be gold."

Sydney started to tremble as the anger evaporated. "What about Chelsea? And my parents? Who was that? Corrin?" She had a good idea, but she needed the words.

"I will not let her hurt you."

"Who was it?" Her voice sounded stronger. She

wasn't some little kid to be shaking at the sight of an intangible person.

"Orlaith."

Sydney closed her eyes. Maybe it would have been better not to have pressed the point. Orlaith! The viper. The woman who had a fondness for putting arrows through people's hearts.

"Sydney?"

"I'm okay." She opened her eyes. She didn't sound okay. "I am okay." That sounded better. Now she had to think of what to do next. A plan. They had to have a plan. "Gold. Where do we get gold from?"

"One of my armbands. As well as the bronze I also have two gold ones. Do you think I can use your parent's workroom?"

Sydney checked her alarm clock. "I guess. They should be well and truly asleep by now."

Corrin turned away to rummage through his gear in her wardrobe. He straightened, a solid gold armband in his hand. "Is there anyone else other than Chelsea and your parents I should make an amulet for?"

Sydney thought of Shawn, but doubted she'd be able to convince him to wear it. Not without a million explanations that he probably wouldn't believe. The last thing she wanted to do was cause him to run a mile in the opposite direction. Besides, he never came to her house. He should be safe. She shook her head. "No." She opened her bedroom door and looked carefully up the hallway. Everything was quiet. "Come on." She kept her voice soft. They crept through the kitchen and dining room, then with a glance in the next hallway, she hurried down it in the direction opposite to her parent's room. She opened the workroom door and turned on the light. "I hope you know what you're doing in here."

Corrin nodded. "I watched your father earlier." He strode to the workbench that was along one wall.

"What will the amulets do?"

"They will stop Orlaith from taking over our bodies."

"She can do that?"

"She is a spirit. They can inhabit living bodies against their will."

"Is that all she can do?"

Corrin paused to stare at her.

Sydney suddenly shook her head, an uneasiness filling her at his expression. "No. Don't tell me. I don't want to hear anymore right now, okay?" Maybe later. Yes, definitely later.

Corrin nodded.

Sydney crossed the room to curl up in the

comfortable armchair in the far corner that was her mum's thinking chair. A small table was beside it with a jar of pencils and a pile of paper, only some of them drawn on. She had barely sat down when she realised her phone was in her room. "I'll be right back. I've got to get my phone."

Corrin nodded, his attention taken up with melting the gold armband.

Sydney watched him a moment longer before she headed to her room. As she reached her door, she felt her nose begin to run and swore under her breath. She grabbed her phone and a couple of tissues. One she pressed to her nose as she hurried back to Corrin. She stopped just inside the room as she watched him wipe at his nose with the back of his hand. Moving to his side, she held out a tissue. "Here."

"Thanks." He didn't look up as he took the tissue.

"Sorry about the nosebleed."

"Probably for the best."

Sydney stared at him with a frown. "What?"

Corrin finally looked up from the clay he was currently kneading. "Blood will make it a stronger amulet."

"Blood will-" Sydney shook her head and held up a hand. "Nope. Don't want to know the details." She curled up in her mum's thinking chair again and checked her phone. She had five missed calls from Chelsea.

Chelsea didn't even bother with a greeting. "Where were you? I've been ringing for ages."

Sydney smiled. The familiar voice eased some of her worries. "Ages, huh?"

"Well, it felt like ages. Anyway. Forget that. Time for the next phase of our plan. My parents said yes providing your parents agreed and no one else goes with us. Dad will be down every second night to collect the boxes we've packed. It's all going into storage closer to the oldies home for when Grandma is well enough to sort through them herself."

"How long will your dad be there? And what do we do with Corrin while he is? I can't even be the length of my own house away from him without a nosebleed. Oh, and the scary viper lady paid us a visit tonight."

"What!"

Sydney pulled the phone away from her ear. "If I wanted to go deaf I'd rather do it by listening to loud music."

"Oh shut up and tell me what's going on."

Sydney couldn't help laughing. She laughed harder when Chelsea promised all kinds of retribution. This is what she had needed, to hear her best friend's voice.

"Okay, okay. Calm down." She took a breath, steeling herself to tell Chelsea about her encounter. When she'd finished telling Chelsea both of them fell silent. "Your phone didn't go flat, did it?"

"No. Sydney, do you think she can hurt people?"

"I don't know. And right now I don't want to know. One disaster at a time please."

"Guys are so stupid. Even in the Dark Ages. Can't they look past a pretty face?"

Sydney chuckled. "I guess not."

"Do you think the amulets will work? I really don't like the thought of her in my body like it's some old coat she's borrowing."

"Can't you ask me something I do know the answer to?"

"It's not my fault you're not very smart."

"Gee thanks." Her tone was dry but she was smiling. "Chelz?"

"Yeah."

"Thanks."

"For?"

"You."

"Aww, don't go getting mushy on me. I hate to cry. It makes my eyes look all puffy and red. Like a pig going to the slaughterhouse."

"Err. Great image there, Chelz. Should I be asking how you know what one looks like?"

It was Chelsea's turn to laugh. "Yeah well don't make me cry then, 'cause it's not a pretty sight. And anyone with an imagination should know what a pig headed for the slaughterhouse looks like. They've got these little piggy eyes in their fat little faces and I bet they're not real happy looking when they learn they're about to become bacon."

"No one has an imagination like yours."

"I always knew I was original."

"Night, Chelz."

"I'll see you tomorrow. You can use the car again, can't you?"

"Yeah. See you at ten-thirty."

She dropped the phone in her lap and watched Corrin. He wore her dad's leather apron, safety glasses and gloves and poured the gold from the crucible into the moulds he'd made out of clay. He held the crucible with tongs and had a larger mould ready for the excess gold. The action seemed so familiar yet very strange since it wasn't her dad she watched. But it still bored her after a few minutes.

"Who was the most famous person in your time?"

Corrin glanced over his shoulder at her. "Why?"

"I want to google them." She picked up her phone again.

"I'll give you a name if you give me an answer."

Sydney grinned. "Okay, what's the question?"

"What does google mean?"

"It's something used to look up information on the internet but sometimes we say it even when we're using other ways of looking up information. I could have said I want to find out about them rather than google them."

"Cunobelinus of the Trinovantes."

Sydney frowned, trying to sound out the name. "Right about now would be a handy time for you to be able to spell," she said when her first guess failed. The second attempt brought up information on a Celtic king who had ruled south Britain around 10 AD to 40 AD. She stared at those dates. Boudica was the only Celtic name she'd known and he'd been alive even before Boudica. "Did you know him?"

"I was fostered with him. Lorcan and I."

"Seriously? And he was a king while you lived with him?"

"Chieftain."

Sydney tapped her phone. "It says here he was a king."

Corrin shrugged. "We called him chieftain of our tribe."

"You're like over two thousand years old." Sydney stared at Corrin as he stepped away from the workbench. "You certainly don't look it."

Corrin grinned as he removed the safety gear. "I don't, huh?" He covered the distance between them and squatted in front of the chair. "How do I look?"

"Stop fishing for compliments." She exited the web page and dropped her phone in her lap.

"Did Chelsea gain the use of her grandma's place?"

"Yeah."

"When do we leave?"

"Monday, I guess. I have to see Shawn tomorrow."

Corrin rose. "Of course. I got in the way of that visit yesterday." He turned back to the workbench and tipped the gold from the moulds into a container of tap water. He took each one out and dried them on a cloth before he pulled a stool over and sat at the workbench.

Sydney watched him engrave the amulets until her eyes would no longer stay open. She didn't know how long she slept in the armchair before she was woken by Corrin carrying her to her room. She looked sleepily up at him, barely making out his features in the shadows. He laid her on the bed and pulled the sheet over her.

"Did you finish them?"

Corrin tilted her head forward and slipped a leather cord over it. When her head was again on her pillow, he pressed the amulet against the skin of her chest below her pulse point. "Go to sleep. You're safe."

"The workroom-"

"It is the same as I found it."

Sydney started to close her eyes again when she remembered. "My phone?"

"Beside you."

She spotted it on her bedside drawers where he pointed. She finally let her eyes close. "Night."

Chapter Twelve

"Now don't forget-" Sydney started to say.

"Enough already," Chelsea said. "How many times do you need to tell us? Anyone'd think we're mentally challenged."

Sydney watched the red light as she waited to drive forward. "Maybe I am."

"No you're not. Everything is going as planned. Your parents agreed to let you help me for a week and we'll take a train there Monday. Someone mentally challenged couldn't have managed that feat," Chelsea said.

"I thought you said we are taking a bus," Corrin said from the backseat.

"A bus to get into the city to catch a train. Then we'll take another bus from the station," Sydney explained.

"All this changing of transport. I miss my horse."

Corrin returned his attention to the world outside his window.

Sydney sent a glare to Corrin through the rear view mirror. He didn't even notice. "I couldn't believe my parents this morning. You should have seen them fawn over Corrin. Anyone'd think those amulets he gave them were priceless jewels. And they even had to get leather cords from their own supplies to be able to wear them."

"You have to admit your plan for him to say it was a thank you for inviting him to dinner was priceless," Chelsea said.

"Yeah, but why couldn't they…" Sydney's voice trailed off and she finished the rest of her words in her head. Be as interested in Shawn. There was nothing wrong with him. So he didn't have a job yet. It was only because the right one hadn't come along. And he had his own fashion sense. Didn't her parents always say you shouldn't follow the crowd?

"Why couldn't they what?" Chelsea asked.

"Never mind. Just don't forget that you invited Corrin today."

"Sydney, enough already." It was Chelsea's turn to glare.

"Okay. I just don't want anything to go wrong. And bringing another guy with you when you visit your boyfriend doesn't sound like the smartest plan," Sydney said.

"Nothing will go wrong," Chelsea said.

"I thought that Friday." Sydney pulled up out the front of Shawn's house that he shared with three other guys. She turned off the engine and stared past Chelsea. The patchy lawn was dotted with crushed purple flowers from the jacaranda tree that was growing on the footpath.

"Today is Sunday. It's a completely different day. Nothing is going to go wrong today," Chelsea said firmly.

"Are we planning to sit in here all day? I do not have much space," Corrin said.

"We're getting out right now." Chelsea swung her door open and turned to Sydney. "Aren't we?"

"Yeah." Sydney didn't sound very certain, but she hopped out of the car and headed for the footpath. She waited till all the doors were closed then pressed the central locking button, sliding the keys into a pocket of her jeans.

When Sydney continued to stand there, Chelsea linked her arm with her friend's. "Come on. Do you want him to look out a window and see you standing out here for no good reason?"

Sydney hurried forward, Corrin on the other side

of Chelsea. She glanced at him, relieved to see he wore a light, long sleeved shirt. She didn't want to have to start the morning out by explaining his scars or having Shawn's housemates giving him too much attention because of them. He still tended to speak a little odd even with all their coaching.

After taking the steps two at a time, Sydney crossed the verandah of the old, highset Queenslander to rap on the closed door. Several minutes passed and she knocked a little louder.

The door was swung open by a man in boxer shorts. His nose had been broken previously and his eyes were partly closed making him look like he was sleepwalking. He turned to yell over his shoulder, "Shawn!"

"Hi Dillon," Sydney said.

"Yeah, whatever." He ambled inside. "Some people sleep days you know. Which is impossible to do when you might as well be banging on the wall of my room."

Sydney followed him, closing the door once they were all inside. "Sorry." Dillon had told her on a previous visit that he worked a late night shift at a local service station. He ambled into the first bedroom, slamming the door shut, leaving them alone in the hallway. She smiled when she saw Shawn open his bedroom door, a black dressing gown loosely belted at the waist.

"It's eleven already?" He yawned, covering his mouth with a hand that had every fingernail painted a different colour and numerous coloured bands around his wrist. His gaze travelled to Chelsea and Corrin.

Sydney hurriedly made introductions. "You've met Chelsea before. This is her friend Corrin."

"I didn't know you were bringing anyone." Shawn leaned against his doorframe.

"I was meant to drop them off at another friend's place, but an emergency came up and she had to go out," Sydney said.

"Whatever. Put the kettle on for me, will you? I'll get dressed." Shawn closed his bedroom door.

"Come on," Sydney muttered as she led the way to the kitchen.

"He didn't seem happy to see us," Chelsea whispered.

Sydney shrugged as she filled the kettle and turned it on. "He just likes a warning."

"Hey, Sydney!"

Sydney grinned as she turned to greet the young man who entered the kitchen. "Marcus. This is my friend Chelsea and her friend Corrin." Marcus was broad shouldered with blond hair that was growing back after being shaved the month before. He was a bouncer at a nightclub and his impressive size was enough to make most troublemakers think twice.

He held out his hand and Sydney was relieved when Chelsea took it first. Why hadn't she thought to explain handshakes to Corrin? How was she meant to think of all these things? It was impossible. Maybe she shouldn't have gone ahead with this plan. No, it was going to work. Somehow they'd get through the day without any problems.

"Hey Syd, you should check out my new sword."

"Marcus collects swords," Sydney hurriedly said when she saw the gleam of interest Corrin showed.

"What type of swords?" Corrin asked.

"All sorts. I'll show you." Marcus bounded from the room without waiting to see if they'd follow.

"He reminds me of an overgrown puppy," Chelsea whispered with a grin.

Sydney laughed. "Come on." She led the way to Marcus' room where an entire wall was almost covered with different types of swords.

Marcus held out a sheathed sword to Sydney. "What do you think?"

Corrin took the sword and pulled it from its scabbard. "It's blunt and unbalanced."

"But it looks good," Marcus said.

"They're for display," Sydney explained. "You know, like hanging a painting on the wall."

"If you're looking for a sword you can use you should talk to Steve. He's in a re-enactment group. He's always practicing for their tournaments." Marcus took back his sword and put his head out the door. "Hey, Steve!"

"Shut up! I'm sleeping," Dillon called out from behind his closed door.

Steve flung his door open and stepped into the hallway. "Yeah, man?" He was wiry with sandy blond hair falling into green eyes.

"I've got you a new practice dummy." Marcus jerked his thumb towards Corrin.

Shawn stepped into the hallway, his black hair gelled to fall in long spikes around his narrow face, bright red shorts that showed the top of green boxers and a black torn t-shirt that had no sleeves. His dark eyes were outlined with eyeliner. "I wouldn't if I was you. The last practice dummy ended up in hospital."

"They're wooden swords. It's not like they're sharp blades," Steve protested.

"I will accept your challenge," Corrin glanced at Sydney. "No matter what the consequences."

Sydney wanted to shout no at him, but knew it

would raise a million questions. Corrin was meant to be Chelsea's friend, not hers. How would it look if she started ordering him around?

"Really?" Steve brightened immediately. "The swords are downstairs. Let's go." He headed for the kitchen and the back door.

Corrin followed, Chelsea and Marcus on his heels. Sydney was torn. She felt her skin tighten and wondered if Corrin was going far enough away to cause a nosebleed. Maybe she should have said no. Didn't he have to follow her orders?

"Don't I get a hello?" Shawn stepped closer, his mouth curving into a smile. "You know the guys were betting you'd bail on me again today."

"Sorry about Friday." She wrapped her arms around Shawn and gave him the greeting he expected. All she wanted to do was run after Corrin and hit him. How dare he do this to her? So what if she'd told him no every time he'd asked about training. That was no excuse. Nausea hit her and she drew away from Shawn. "I haven't made your coffee yet."

"Forget the coffee. We've practically got the house to ourselves." Shawn tugged her towards his room.

"But I've never seen a sword fight before." She looked towards the kitchen.

"It's not a real sword fight." Shawn's hand gripped hers more tightly as he took another step towards his room. "Come on."

"But I-" Sydney again looked in the direction of the kitchen. Her head pounded and she couldn't think clearly. "I've never even seen a pretend sword fight. And a movie doesn't count."

Shawn dropped her hand. "I thought you came over here to see me today."

"I did. I have. How long can a fight last?"

"Whatever." Shawn brushed past her and headed for the kitchen.

Chapter Thirteen

Sydney followed Shawn to the kitchen, the pain easing a little. This wasn't what she'd expected of the day. She could kill Corrin. Okay, maybe not kill him, she wasn't suicidal, but he better look out when they left. This was meant to be her day, not his.

"Well? Aren't you going downstairs?" Shawn grabbed milk from the fridge and a mug from the draining rack.

"I guess." She hesitated. "Are you coming down too?"

Shawn shrugged and continued to make his coffee.

Sydney watched him a moment longer before the pain made her hurry to the back door. She was halfway down the stairs when Corrin looked behind him and met her gaze. She knew he would have felt her arrive from the lessening of pain. He stood next to Steve in the middle of the dusty backyard, well away from the rusty Hills Hoist clothes line that leaned to one side and was missing most of its wire lines. He pulled off his shirt and threw it to Chelsea.

Marcus, who sat on the bottom step, swore. He called out, "Hey Corrin, what the hell happened to you?"

"Car accident." Sydney sat beside Marcus.

Marcus swore again. "You look like you were put through a shredder."

"Shut up, Marcus. Can't you see I'm trying to tell him the rules here?" Steve gave Corrin a wooden sword.

"I can tell him the rules," Marcus said. "Don't get hurt like the last one."

Steve glared at Marcus. "It was a little splinter."

"Little! It was like a foot long," Marcus said.

"An inch. One measly inch. A pair of tweezers would have got it out. But no, he had to go running off to the hospital. I'm surprised he didn't call an ambulance," Steve complained.

Corrin swung the wooden sword several times. It was a bit shorter than the sword, but he looked just as comfortable with it. "Is that all the rules?"

Steve turned back to him. "Yeah." He swung at Corrin with his sword and within less than a minute, his sword was on the ground and Corrin was grinning. Steve swore. "What the hell was that? Give me a chance, man." He picked up his sword. Once more it took less than a minute for Corrin to disarm him.

"Again?" Corrin gestured towards the wooden sword lying in the dirt.

"What's the problem, Steve? Did you get a splinter?" Shawn leaned on the rail at the top of the steps. "Nice to see you're the one losing for a change. We always knew you weren't as good as you reckon you are."

Steve pulled his phone from his back pocket and pointed to Corrin. "Don't go anywhere." He dialled a number. "Bob, get your arse over here now. You're not going to believe this. Hell, call the whole group." There was a pause while Steve listened. "Man you're going to regret it if you don't." He laughed. "Sure. See you soon." Steve returned his phone to his pocket and picked up his sword. "Let's do this again."

Seven more times Corrin disarmed Steve. Marcus and Shawn called out comments that cast doubt on Steve's skills, but he didn't pay them the slightest bit of attention. Before Steve had a chance to pick up his sword again, a man walked down the side of the house and into the backyard. He was over six foot, bearded and his brown hair was tied back in a short ponytail.

"Bob, this dude's awesome. You've just gotta take him on, man." Steve picked up his sword and handed it to Bob.

Bob eyed Corrin. "You look like you've been sliced by a thousand blades."

"Car accident," Corrin said.

Bob shrugged. "Doesn't matter. Show me what you've got."

With a nod, Corrin attacked. Bob lasted longer than Steve, but he was soon disarmed. Corrin waited for him to collect his sword from the ground and then attacked again. Within the hour, the backyard was filled with Steve's re-enactment mates and they were each taking turns trying to disarm Corrin. By the end of another hour Corrin was giving them fighting tips.

When Marcus left the bottom step to go inside, Chelsea came and sat beside Sydney. "I can't believe he's doing this to you." She glanced at Corrin.

Sydney sighed, keeping her voice low. "Yeah, but look at him. That's him. That's who he is."

"What do you mean?"

"That torc he wears. You know what my mum said about it?"

Chelsea shook her head.

"It's the same as those worn by important men. Or kings."

"He was a king?"

Sydney stared at Corrin. "I don't know. But I do know he was raised by one."

"So he's a prince?"

"I wouldn't have a clue. I'm not exactly sure how things worked back then. But I do know he was a lot more important than he is in our time. Here he's just another kid. But right this minute, he's a warrior and everyone in this yard recognises that. Even the guys that are a lot older than him. They're treating him like he's their leader. Like they look up to him." Her gaze was drawn back to Corrin. He swung his sword at the man he currently faced, his body graceful. Sweat beaded on his skin catching in the sunlight as he moved. Seconds after he disarmed his opponent another stepped forward. Without hesitation Corrin attacked. "This is who he is. A warrior. Maybe a prince or a king. But he wasn't some teenager just starting out. I can't believe he lets me order him around like I've been doing."

"Sydney."

She turned to see Shawn was back outside on the top step again. She rose to her feet and headed upstairs to stand next to him. "This place is packed."

"Yeah. Great. It's a circus." He dismissed the crowd with a wave of his hand. "You coming inside?"

"I don't know. I was going to ask you to come and watch with me." She could almost see the end coming. Unlike Friday she wasn't frantically trying to think of a way to prevent it. Her fingers went to the medallion around her neck and rubbed at the pattern on it. There was only so much she could deal with at a time. Her heart lurched and the nausea she felt wasn't just from the distance she stood from Corrin.

"I thought you were here to spend time with me."

"I am."

"Look, I don't need no dramas in my life. I moved out of home to get away from them." Shawn rested his hip against the railing.

"I'm sorry you feel that way, but maybe you're right." Sydney turned to go back to Chelsea.

Shawn grabbed her arm, tugging on it until she faced him. "Are you ditching me?"

"No. I thought you were ditching me. That's what it sounded like to me. And you're probably right. I'm not even going to be in town for the next week."

"Since when?"

"My parents told me this morning. I think they know that I'm sneaking around to see you." Sydney knew perfectly well her parents didn't, but it sounded good. And maybe it was better to end things now instead of dragging them out. Even though her heart screamed no, it wasn't time, her mind said the opposite.

Shawn stared at her a moment longer then linked his fingers with hers. "Sure. Let's watch the idiots beat each other up with toy swords." He walked down the steps with her and they sat, two above Chelsea.

Sydney's mind was a whirl. What had just happened? Hadn't he been about to break up with her? She could have sworn he was. Now he was sitting next to her watching an activity he'd spent an hour mocking. What the hell was going on? She guessed they were still together otherwise he wouldn't be sitting next to her with his arm around her. His other hand dropped onto her thigh and started making lazy movements. When he started nuzzling at her neck she was certain they were still together.

She turned towards him, wanting answers. "Shawn-" he cut off her words with a kiss. Days ago she'd looked forward to every single kiss. Now she was only confused. A collective groan from the crowd behind them caused her to draw away from Shawn.

"Ignore them." Shawn tried to pull her back to him.

Sydney resisted. "It looks like some of them are headed this way."

Chelsea stood up. "The fights are over. We better get out of the way before we're trampled."

Sydney saw that Corrin led the group headed for the stairs. She quickly rose to her feet and looked down at Shawn until he did the same. He dropped his arm around her shoulders and they walked up the stairs. Sydney could feel Corrin's distance from her by the slight tightening and release of her skin as he followed her.

When they reached the kitchen, Sydney stopped. "I need a drink of water."

Before Shawn could argue, Steve called out, "Grab one for Corrin too. Did you all see him out there? Man, take a seat. You must be exhausted."

Corrin sat at the kitchen table and Sydney grabbed the cold water from the fridge and two glasses.

"I'll have a drink too," Shawn said.

She grabbed a third glass and filled them, handing one to Shawn first since he'd joined her at the bench. Without a word she gave Corrin his drink.

He took a mouthful and frowned. "It's cold."

Sydney snatched the glass from him and tipped the water down the sink and filled it with tap water. "Here." She shoved the glass back at him. "Now it's not." She was tempted to tip the water over him. Her hands curled into fists as she struggled not to do something stupid. Something that would have Shawn asking questions she couldn't answer.

Corrin had a mouthful then nodded. "Thank you."

Steve sat at the table across from Corrin. "Where did you learn to fight like that?"

"My father and foster father."

"You were in foster care?" Steve asked.

Worried Corrin would say the wrong thing, Sydney quickly answered. "No, a relative who took him in after his parents died."

"Both your parents? Man, that's harsh," Steve said.

"How did you know?" Shawn asked.

"Chelsea told me," Sydney said.

Dillon appeared in the kitchen doorway. "I'm trying to sleep. You have all heard of it haven't you? Oh that's right, it's something you think I don't need."

"Sorry man, but you should have seen this dude use a sword. I don't think any of the characters in my entire action movie collection could beat him," Steve said.

"Of course they couldn't. They're actors. If they didn't have someone choreograph the moves for them they'd look like they were trying to fight their way out of a wet paper bag. Now can't you do something quieter?"

"We could watch a movie," Steve suggested.

"Good. But use mute." Dillon spun on his heel and stalked down the hallway.

Steve called after him. "That defeats the purpose." He turned back to the handful of people crowding the kitchen. "Movie anyone?"

"My pick. You chose last time." Marcus bounded towards the lounge room.

Steve followed arguing, then shouted over his shoulder, "Come on Corrin. You don't want to miss the start."

Chapter Fourteen

Sydney continued to lean against the bench as the kitchen rapidly emptied. She watched Shawn as he slowly smiled and put his glass aside. He rested his hands on her hips.

"What say we skip the movie?"

Sydney put her own glass on the bench. "I guess." Maybe she should go home. This was so much harder than she'd thought it would be.

Shawn laughed. "You playing hard to get?" He linked his fingers through hers and tugged her towards his room again. "Hurry up before something else distracts you."

Sydney managed to contain her annoyance at his comment. But the rest of the afternoon didn't go as planned. It started out fine. But before the movie ended they argued and Sydney stormed out of Shawn's room and he slammed the door behind her.

The only person who glanced her way was Corrin. She looked away from him to find a place to sit on the opposite side of the room.

Shawn was wrong. She wasn't a tease. They'd only known each other a month. What did he want? For her to have hopped into bed with him on the first day they'd met? She stewed all through the movie and when it was over, it was time for them to go. She had to get the car home.

Steeling herself, Sydney knocked on Shawn's door. "I have to go."

He didn't bother to open the door. "Yeah, sure. See you next time. Maybe without your entourage."

Sydney felt her cheeks heat. Embarrassment was quickly followed by anger that caused more heat to rise in her cheeks. "If you're lucky."

The door swung open and Shawn tugged her forward. "I'm kidding." He kissed her before he let her go. "Ring me."

Sydney could only nod, still angry. She headed for the front door, Chelsea beside her, Corrin following.

Steve hurried after them to shove a scrap of paper at Corrin. "Ring any time you want a rematch. And the group would love to have you join us. We meet up the last Sunday of every month, in full gear. You don't have to come kitted out straight away. You've got time to get your gear together."

Sydney couldn't help grinning. Corrin could arrive in clothes that were more authentic than what any of them owned. "Is that a date?"

Marcus laughed from behind them. "You gonna kiss him goodbye too?"

Steve gestured towards Marcus with his middle finger and told him were to go before he faced Corrin. "I'm serious, man. Any time you want a rematch, give me a yell."

Corrin nodded. "Thank you. It was a good fight."

"On your part maybe."

"No. You picked up what I showed you quickly. You need more practice. It is not something that can be learned in a day. You would have been able to live by your sword if you'd been born in the Dark Ages."

Steve looked surprised. "Ya reckon?"

Corrin nodded before he followed Sydney and Chelsea out the front door.

Once they were in the car, Sydney said, "That was nice of you to say that to Steve. They all tease him about being into re-enacting."

"It wasn't nice. It was the truth."

The car was filled with silence all the way to Chelsea's house. The silence was momentarily broken by their goodbyes and returned again as Sydney drove home. She locked the car the moment Corrin was out and watched as he slipped around the side of the house. She used the front door key hanging with the car keys and again reminded herself she needed to get one cut for herself.

After she let Corrin in her sliding door, she dropped the keys on the kitchen bench and called out, "I'm home."

"Come here a minute, Sydney."

"I need to use the bathroom." She took a step towards the front hallway. How would she explain a nosebleed to her mum?

Victoria came out of the back hallway. "You're on your own? Chelsea's not coming over tonight?"

"No."

"What about Corrin?"

Sydney grinned. "I knew you wanted to adopt him."

"Why couldn't you date a nice boy like him instead of wanting to see someone like Shawn?"

"Is this talk going to take long? I really need to use the bathroom." She didn't, but since she'd already used that excuse she thought she better stick with it.

"Have you eaten?"

Sydney nodded. "I'm fine." She hadn't eaten, but

didn't think she could after her afternoon. She didn't even want to think about what a fail it had been. Maybe she'd have a snack later.

"Behave while you're away. Don't go doing anything silly. Like inviting Shawn to join you."

"As if. It's girl time."

Victoria stared at her a moment longer. "I'll leave some cash on the kitchen bench for you when we leave in the morning so you can buy food. I want you to ring us every day and let us know how you're doing."

"Every day! Mum!"

"Every day." Victoria's tone was firm.

"Fine."

"And make sure you take plenty of sunscreen."

Sydney grinned. "You aren't going to remind me to pack clean underwear too, are you?"

Victoria closed the distance between them and wrapped her arms around her. "You're my baby. The house is going to be quiet without you."

"I thought that would be a good thing. Don't you always complain I have my music up too loud? And that I'll end up killing the speakers of your stereo."

Victoria let her go and tapped her on the nose. "Take care, love."

"I will." Sydney paused a beat. "Now can I use the bathroom?"

"Go on then."

Sydney could feel her mum's gaze on her as she retreated to her bedroom. She leaned on the door once she closed it, her forehead pressed against the timber. When the tightness of her skin completely eased, she knew Corrin must be directly behind her.

"Are you okay?"

Sydney faced him. "What do you think?"

"I think it is probably safer for me if I do not try and guess how you are feeling."

"I had a fight with my boyfriend, which is probably understandable since I spent the morning watching another guy instead of spending time with him. My mum thinks you're who I really should be dating and your evil sister has issues with me. Is that enough or do you want more?"

"Orlaith has issues with me too and Shawn isn't worth worrying about."

"He's my boyfriend," Sydney hissed when she would have preferred to scream the words.

"Then maybe you should listen to your mum. He doesn't treat you like he should."

"And how should he treat me? How would you do things differently?"

"I would ask you what you want."

"And you think that'd work?"

"It worked for Lorcan."

Sydney brushed past him, needing to put more space between them. "Yeah, that worked out real well. Didn't she run off after a year?"

"That's when Lorcan decided it was time to tell Orlaith what he wanted."

"Which was?"

"Children. But she didn't want to ruin her figure and risk her life for children so she ran and lied to me about why she ran." Corrin took a step towards her. "He was playing with you, Sydney. Every time you backed away, he was interested. When you came close he pushed you away. You don't want someone who'll play with your feelings like that."

"He's moody sometimes."

Corrin shook his head. "No. He needs to be in control of the relationship. And he needs to be the centre of it. You can do better than him."

"Like who? You?"

"No. Better. As you keep pointing out to me, I don't have the knowledge for your world. You deserve a lot better than either of us."

Sydney had to look away. "You're learning more every day."

"But not enough."

The sliding door rattled like someone was trying to get in. Sydney stared at it until the noise died down. "What are we going to do about Orlaith?"

"Why don't we work on the problem of the great service I need to do for you first?"

"Yeah well, I have no clue what a great service is and we have less than two weeks to deal with it. Unless you think you can manage high school."

"Would I need those letters and numbers you are so fond of?"

Sydney nodded.

"Then we need to find a great service for me to complete."

Sydney's phone rang and when she looked at the display she was surprised to see it was Shawn. "Hi."

"Where are you going for the week?"

Sydney sat on the edge of her bed. "To help Chelsea pack up her grandma's house. She's in an old people's home and no one else has time to deal with it so we're stuck doing it."

"On your own? No adults?"

"On our own."

"Where abouts is it?"

Sydney gave him the address, then wondered why he wanted it. "Why?"

"Maybe I'll come and visit."

"Chelsea's dad is calling in to see us every second night starting with Tuesday. Maybe you better ring first in case he changes his days."

"Is that the only reason I should ring first? You're not hiding anything from me, are you?"

"Our parents told us we couldn't have visitors while we stayed there." Sydney watched as Corrin returned to his alphabet DVD.

"You sound like you don't want me to visit."

She couldn't help but think of Corrin's comments about the way Shawn acted. But what did he know? He'd grown up in the Dark Ages. Things were different back then. "What about Wednesday?"

"I don't know. I'll have to see what I'm doing. I'll ring you. Night."

"Night." Sydney stared at her phone. Was Corrin right? Was it all a game to Shawn? She dropped backwards to lie on her bed, her feet still on the floor. She had no clue. It wasn't like she'd had a heap of boyfriends to be able to compare his behaviour to. He was the fourth and they'd all been different. Why did things have to be so complicated? Couldn't people just say exactly how they felt? She tried to ignore the thought that entered her mind, but it snuck in anyway. Like you do?

She rolled over and looked at the alarm clock. Nearly eight. It was time to call it a night. This day had been a bust so it was probably a good idea to end it. Sydney dropped her phone on the bedside drawers and retreated to the bathroom with a singlet and pair of cotton shorts. There was no way she was going to wear pyjamas while Corrin slept in her room. Or one of the lacy nighties Chelsea had given her for her last birthday.

Chapter Fifteen

They quickly fell into a routine once they arrived at Chelsea's grandma's house. Mornings were spent at the beach and they called into the supermarket on their walk home to grab some groceries for the day. Corrin had been like a little kid in a toy store the first day they'd visited the supermarket. It had made Sydney smile.

After lunch they packed some boxes then lazed around, watching a couple of movies before they walked to the beach again. More boxes were packed before dinner and the evening usually ended with another movie. Chelsea's dad only stayed an hour Tuesday night and Corrin spent that time crouched under the house that was four steps up off the ground.

Even though Sydney felt bad about sending him under there, he waved her apologies away with a grin, telling her he'd been in worse places. Sydney almost asked him about those places, but decided she didn't want to know what the Harbinger of Death considered worse than a spider infested, cramped, dark space.

Wednesday came and went with no sign of Shawn. The only other visitor they had was Orlaith. The first few visits had been worrying until they realised she had been able to do nothing other than stir up a strong wind.

Friday lunch found them crowded around Sydney's phone to see the results of her search on a great service. She frowned as she read through them. "They all seem to be about customer service. I really don't think that's what will solve our problem."

"This one is about missionary work." Chelsea pointed to the site listed at the bottom of the page.

"Somehow I don't think that's it either." Sydney turned to Corrin. "You're not being very helpful."

"I already told you what was considered a great service in my time."

"Save my life, fight an army, go on a quest." Sydney touched a finger for each point. "You are so not helping."

"You forgot win you untold treasures," Corrin said.

"You're still not helping."

Chelsea glanced towards the front door. "Was that a car? I hope Dad isn't making a surprise visit."

"I'll run and tidy up the blankets on my floor that Corrin is sleeping on. Corrin you wait in the laundry in case you have to hide underneath the house again." Sydney headed for the bedroom she shared with Corrin. It didn't take her long to tidy up and she was back in the living room in time to see Shawn step through the front door.

"It's Shawn," Chelsea said when Sydney continued to stare at him.

"You said you'd ring," Sydney finally managed to say.

"I thought I'd surprise you." He glanced around the nearly empty room. "It's just the two of you here?"

Sydney shook her head. "No. Corrin is visiting too." She raised her voice. "Corrin, it isn't Chelsea's dad." She turned as Corrin stepped into the kitchen.

"What's he doing here?" Shawn glared at Corrin.

"Chelsea invited him. This is her grandma's house."

Chelsea moved away from where she'd been standing near the front door and linked her arm with Corrin's. "Come on. You can help me do some more packing in Grandma's room." She led the way to the room she was staying in and closed the door behind them.

Silence filled the room as Sydney continued to stare at Shawn, her skin having tightened when Corrin left the room.

"Aren't you even going to say hello?"

Anger, confusion and uncertainty swirled inside her. "Hello."

Shawn crossed the room to stand in front of her. "You're usually more enthusiastic when you see me." He rested his hands on her hips. "Did you miss me?"

Sydney pulled away. "You said you'd ring."

Shawn's smile disappeared. "You're not going to harp on about that are you? I'm here. Isn't that better?"

"No. I like to know what's going on. You told me five days ago you'd ring."

"You could have rung me."

"Why?" Sydney's hands went to her hips, anger flaring. "So you can play more games?"

"Don't be stupid."

"I'm not being stupid. I'd have to be stupid not to notice." She ignored the fact she hadn't noticed and it had been Corrin who'd pointed it out to her. "I'm sick of feeling like a game to you. I get close, you push me away. I move away, you pull me back. What's with that? It's over. I won't put up with not knowing where I stand." With every word she spoke she ignored the thoughts that circled her mind demanding what she was doing and telling her to shut up and not let him go. Corrin was right. She deserved to be treated better than this. Even if she wasn't sure she really wanted to let him go.

"Over? But it can't be." Shawn looked stunned. "I don't want it to be over."

"Then you shouldn't have kept playing these games."

"When I don't, girls dump me. They complain I'm too possessive. You can't really mean it."

"Yeah, I do. I like to know where I stand."

"You should have said sooner. Now that I know-"

"Forget it. It's too late."

"It can't be." Shawn reached out towards her.

Sydney stepped to the side, her gaze momentarily drawn to the closed bedroom door across from her. "It's too late."

Shawn turned to face her. "It's because of Corrin, isn't it? I've seen how you look at him."

"No. It's because of how you've treated me. I'm not a toy. Not some yo-yo you can throw away and pull back whenever you feel like it. The string has finally broken and I'm outta here."

"No you're not." Shawn grabbed her by the upper arm.

"Let go of me." Sydney tried to pull away and froze when she saw the misty shape of a woman standing behind Shawn. "Orlaith?"

Chelsea's door burst open and Corrin stood in the doorway. "Let her go." He strode forward, forcing his way through the misty figure. Orlaith evaporated before Shawn could turn and see her.

"I knew it." Shawn pushed Sydney from him and glared at her. "You're seeing him behind my back."

"No, I'm not." She turned away. "Just forget it, Shawn. I'm sure this is all too much of a drama for you." Sydney stared at the kitchen bench as the room behind her remained silent.

"You're right. You're not worth the hassle." The front door slammed behind Shawn and moments later they heard his car start up.

Corrin rested his hand on her shoulder. "Sydney? Are you okay?"

She turned to face him. "Still not game to guess?"

Corrin smiled slightly. "I am not feeling suicidal today."

Sydney couldn't return his smile. "Does it make me a bad person that I feel relieved he's gone?" Her words were a whisper. It wasn't the only feeling, but it was the one that was strongest. She just couldn't cope with any extra problems at the moment. Orlaith was enough of a drama without adding any more.

"No. I think you probably stuck with him longer than you normally would, because someone told you not to." He grinned. "I can understand how that could happen." He took a step closer. "How about I help you take your mind off him?"

"Is that what you think of me? That I go from one guy to the next?"

"I know you do not. You forget I'm one of the few people who know for certain you're a virgin."

"Then what?"

"I was teasing. Joking. I was only going to suggest a movie."

"Don't you think I've had enough of games?"

"You want truth? No games?" Corrin stepped close enough that his body touched hers. His head descended until their lips barely met.

Sydney tried to hang onto her anger, telling herself she should move away from him. Instead her arms twined around his neck, her body pressed closer to his. The warmth of his arms surrounded her. Sydney buried her fingers in Corrin's hair as his arms tightened around her. A blast of air buffeted them, dragging Sydney partially back to her surroundings.

Corrin turned slightly, his arms still holding

Sydney. "Get away, Orlaith. If you were more than mist I'd drive a sword through your heart."

The misty figure drew back an equally misty bow and let loose an arrow that evaporated on the air. Her expression was a mixture of anger and defiance.

Sydney stared at Orlaith and tried to take a step away from Corrin. "Does she seem more together? Less misty?" She finally managed to take a step back, but she couldn't bring herself to look in Corrin's direction. What the hell had she been thinking? Obviously she hadn't been.

"I don't know."

"If I was more than mist I would put an arrow through your heart, Corrin."

Chelsea ran into the room. "She spoke? The viper spoke? Did I hear her speak?"

Sydney could only nod.

"She's getting stronger?" Chelsea's gaze remained on Orlaith.

"Of course I am you pathetic little child."

"I think I preferred her when she couldn't talk." Sydney stepped forward and swept her arm through the mist, forcing Orlaith to break up into swirls.

"This cannot be good." Corrin dragged his gaze from Orlaith to Sydney. "I knew I should have brought my sword."

Sydney met Corrin's gaze. Her gaze momentarily dropped to his lips before she forced it upwards again and her attention on the correct subject. "Impossible. If you'd been caught wandering around with that you'd have ended up in jail." Sydney gestured towards Orlaith who paced the room. "Forget about her. We need to figure out what to do about breaking our bond."

"You can do that while you help me pack. Dad will be here tomorrow night and we haven't got enough done." Chelsea headed back into her grandma's room.

With a last glance at Orlaith, Sydney started to follow. Corrin reached out a hand and stopped her. She stared at his fingers wrapped around hers. When he continued to stand there quietly, she slowly moved her gaze until she met his.

"No games?"

Sydney shook her head. "I think I'll stick with the games after all. Nothing happened."

Corrin reached out and ran his thumb over her bottom lip, his other hand still holding hers. "Play all the games you want. I know the truth." Letting go of her hand, he headed after Chelsea.

Chapter Sixteen

Sydney stared after Corrin. What was she going to do? Things were barely over with Shawn. The last thing she needed was to start another relationship. And what about once he'd done his great service? She closed her eyes and took a deep breath. Nothing had happened. It had been a simple kiss. Okay, maybe not simple, but it had only been one kiss.

Chelsea called out, "Get in here and help. We're not doing all the work, Sydney."

Another deep breath and Sydney forced herself to join them. By early evening, they'd packed nearly everything, none of them feeling up to the beach while Orlaith hounded them. There was only the kitchenware they were still using.

Chelsea watched Corrin add the last box to the stack in the laundry. "How about a movie? I think we need to laze about for a while. We've outdone ourselves."

"What about dinner?" Sydney asked.

"We could always order pizza," Chelsea suggested.

"This is the pizza you said a fork wasn't good for?" Corrin asked.

"Yeah." Before Sydney could agree with Chelsea's suggestion, there was a knock at the front door. It was quickly followed by the sound of a thunk. "What-"

"Orlaith!" Corrin ran into the living room. "I'm going to break that bow in two."

Sydney and Chelsea followed, stopping as they saw the arrow imbedded in the front door. Sydney grabbed hold of Chelsea, speechless.

Orlaith laughed, becoming mist. "You cannot break what you cannot hold. You lose again, Corrin."

There was another knock at the door. A longer, more impatient sound. No one but Orlaith moved. She paced back and forth, her bow drawn. "Who shall I shoot first? One of you, or maybe the company?"

Corrin ran across the room and flung the door open. "Shawn." He continued to stand in the doorway. "What are you doing here?"

"I want to see Sydney." Shawn tried to push his way into the house.

"Corrin! Look out." Sydney raced forward as Orlaith fired another arrow.

Corrin launched himself at Shawn, throwing him to the ground. They landed on the verandah.

Orlaith slammed the door behind them and with a laugh spun to face Sydney and Chelsea. "What is it you told your mum, Sydney? It's just us girls. We're having girl time." She slowly walked towards them, her bow at her side, an arrow in the other hand. "What do we do for girl time? I remember now. We invite boys over and kiss them." Orlaith laughed again, her voice loud enough to be heard outside. "But I guess we cannot do that. They are both busy banging on the door."

Sydney reached out and took Chelsea's hand, taking a step backwards towards the kitchen. "Then why don't you let them in?"

Orlaith acted as if Sydney hadn't spoken. She continued to stalk forward. "I know what we can do. We can talk about boys and kisses instead. Remind me what it is like to kiss Corrin. It has been such a very long time since I have kissed him."

The banging on the door increased. "Open this door before I break it down, Orlaith," Corrin shouted. There was a moment of silence before Corrin warned, "Enough, Shawn."

Sydney continued to back away from Orlaith, her fingers going numb from her tight grip on Chelsea's hand.

"Sydney! Is she telling the truth? What's going on with you and Corrin?" Shawn demanded. His face appeared pressed against the window to the right of the front door. "Who the hell is she? What's going on in there, Sydney?"

Orlaith raised her bow. "We are having fun. Do you want to join us, Shawn?" She laughed when Sydney dropped behind the bench, pulling Chelsea with her. "I would not hurt you, Sydney. I am sure we are going to be such good friends. Besides, if I tried to kill you, Corrin would only save you and break his curse. That would ruin all my fun. No, I will make do with the other one for a plaything. What do you call her again?" Orlaith waited as if someone would answer. When the only sound was the banging on the front door, she spoke again. "Chelsea. I think I will have a lot of fun with Chelsea before I finally put her out of her misery."

"Corrin, protect Chelsea," Sydney called out, still pressed against the bench, the handle of one of the cupboards digging into her back. Chelsea was tucked against her side. She didn't dare move.

Orlaith came around the edge of the bench, her

bow drawn, an arrow aimed at them. "You really do not want to upset me, little girl. I will have one of them tonight and you cannot ask Corrin to protect the world. That would not work. You would have to care for the person being saved for it to be a great service. Care for them as much as you care for yourself. And I know you do not care for the boy. Or you would not have been crawling all over Corrin today."

Shawn swore. "I knew it. I knew there was something going on between you two. That's why you ended things, isn't it?"

Sydney continued to stare at the arrow pointed at her as she turned her body to shelter Chelsea better. Would the arrow pierce the two of them? Or would bone and muscle stop it from travelling through to Chelsea? Sydney shuddered.

"Stay. Very. Still." Orlaith's voice was a whisper. "I wonder if I have lost any of my skill." She moved her aim slightly to the left.

Everything seemed so quiet Sydney could hear her breath. Her heart beat. Or was it Chelsea's breath, Chelsea's heartbeat? They came so fast. A rush of air passed her cheek and she blinked, wishing she could close her eyes and keep them closed. Instead she watched as Orlaith drew yet another arrow. Behind her, Sydney felt Chelsea press harder against her, as if they would blend into one. Her breath caught on a sob.

"Hmm. I do not think that was a good enough test of my skill. Maybe I should try to get a little closer with the next one." Orlaith tapped the arrowhead against her lip. She smiled, pressed a kiss against the metal and notched the arrow. "Remember. Very, very still." Her voice was so soft it was almost a breath of air.

Sydney's body trembled. Or maybe it was Chelsea's. Possibly both of them. She could no longer tell. She wanted to run. Instead, she forced herself to stillness. A rush of air above her registered before she realised there was no arrow in Orlaith's hand. Sydney leapt to her feet, dragging Chelsea with her as she ran for the back door. Orlaith's laughter followed. She slammed into Corrin as she rounded the corner into the laundry, his hands tightening on her before he pushed them behind him. She stopped as she spotted Shawn at the back door, an accusation in his eyes.

Corrin stood between them and Orlaith. "Get out. All of you. The beach. Now."

"How sweet. You think sacrificing yourself will end the curse and me? It does not work like that. I am free. No matter how things end for you, I am free. I am real, or I will be soon enough. There is nothing you can do about it, Corrin." Orlaith stepped close enough that she could pat his cheek lightly. "You were always the fool."

"And you always underestimated people." Corrin pushed her hand away. "Getting rid of you would be a great service." He raised his voice. "What do you say, Sydney?"

"Yes. Find a way to get rid of the viper." Sydney huddled at the door with Chelsea, Shawn behind them. "We have a saying around here. The only good snake is a dead one." Her voice was strong and steady, not giving away how terrified she was.

"Done." Corrin backed away from Orlaith.

"You have no idea how to do this. You are not clever enough, Corrin." Orlaith pressed a kiss against another arrow. "I do not have to kill you to put you out of action." She smiled as she notched her arrow.

"Corrin!" Sydney started forward only to be dragged back by Chelsea and Shawn.

Corrin moved before the arrow left Orlaith's hands. He pushed them out the back door and pulled Sydney with him towards the front of the house. He paused when he saw Shawn's car. He turned to Shawn who had followed. "Drive us to the beach."

"What for?" Shawn glanced over his shoulder. There was no sign of Orlaith.

"Safety." Corrin pulled Sydney towards the car, Chelsea close behind since the two still clasped hands.

Sydney looked at Shawn who continued to stand at the front of the car, staring at them. "Come on. We have to get out of here before Orlaith follows."

The front door swung open. "Did someone call me? Do you miss me already?" Orlaith laughed. "You should see your faces. What is that silly comment you have in this time? Yes. Priceless." She laughed, throwing her head back. "Priceless."

Sydney swung the driver's door open and seeing the keys in the ignition, slid in.

Shawn ran over and grabbed hold of the door before Sydney could close it. "What do you think you're doing?"

"Get in or get left behind." Sydney started the car.

"You can't steal my car." Shawn grabbed her shoulder and tried to drag her from the car. His hands dropped from her as an arrow flew past him. He swore and turned towards Orlaith. "Who the hell do you think you are, bitch?"

Orlaith, completely solid looking, took a step forward as she notched another arrow. "Why do you not come over here and find out?"

"Get in the bloody car before I leave you here for her." Sydney put the car in reverse. "Now!"

Chapter Seventeen

Shawn hesitated. He glanced between Sydney and Orlaith. When Sydney slowly drove backwards, he pulled the back door open and jumped in. The moment the doors were closed, she swung hard as she pressed down on the accelerator. "Where'd you learn to drive? Slow down!"

"Shut up," Sydney muttered as she headed for the beach, with frequent glances in the rear view mirror. She shot a look at Corrin who sat beside her. "What's the beach got that'll protect us?"

"Salt."

"What?"

"Salt. In the water."

Sydney shook her head and still his comment made no more sense. "Keep it four-year-old simple."

"Salt protects you from evil spirits. She cannot cross a line of salt, or a body of water filled with salt."

Chelsea leaned forward, her hand clutching the back of the driver's seat. "People have salt in them."

"Not enough," Corrin said.

"That sounds like some stupid myth," Shawn said.

"Then that's probably what we need since Orlaith is some stupid myth." Sydney couldn't resist another long look in the rear view mirror. Where was Orlaith? Surely she wasn't going to give up that easily.

"We're going to spend the night in the ocean?" Chelsea asked.

"Whatever it takes," Sydney muttered. "She's not going to win." Again she glanced in the rear view mirror. Where was Orlaith? What was she planning?

"What about our parents? We need to ring our parents," Chelsea said.

Sydney fumbled for her phone. "Ring them now." She glanced between her phone and the road, her gaze scanning for police. She didn't want to get caught talking on her phone while she was driving, but she also didn't want to risk standing around on the beach waiting for Orlaith. When her phone rang out, Sydney swore and redialled. "Pick up," she muttered while she listened to Chelsea talk to her own parents from the backseat.

"Sydney? Why are you ringing so early? Is something wrong?"

Sydney couldn't speak for a moment. "No. We thought we'd have an early night. We want to see the sunrise at the beach tomorrow." She used the excuse she'd heard Chelsea give.

"Are you sure everything's okay? You sound… I don't know, upset?"

Sydney nodded and swallowed even though she knew her mum couldn't see her. "Sad movie. You know what it's like."

"Which one?"

"Ahh…" She tried to think of the last movie she'd seen her mum cry over. "The Notebook." Sydney parked the car. "Well, I was just ringing to say goodnight."

"Goodnight, love."

Sydney turned off her phone and dropped it on the passenger floor along with her t-shirt and shorts she'd wriggled out of. She was glad that, like Chelsea, she still had her bikini on. Once out of the car, she handed the keys to Shawn who hid them.

They silently walked into the ocean, Chelsea and Sydney with an arm around each other. Shawn walked on the other side of Sydney while Corrin followed behind, his gaze scanning the area.

"How far do we need to go?" Knee deep, Sydney turned to face the shore.

"A lot further. Her arrows can still reach us here," Corrin said.

By the time Sydney was chest deep in the ocean, Orlaith was pacing the beach screaming at them. Sydney couldn't stop staring at Orlaith. "What do we do now? And how long will we be stuck in here?"

"Till dawn."

Sydney turned her gaze on Corrin, her mouth ajar. "Dawn! Damn it!" She struck out at Corrin who grabbed her fist. She glared at him. "Let me go."

"Then stop trying to attack me. You were the one who chose to set me free."

"I didn't know!" Sydney pulled away from Corrin.

"What's going on? Who is she?" Shawn gestured towards Orlaith, still pacing the beach, who was quiet now. "And what is going on between you two? Is he why you broke up with me?" Shawn jerked his head towards Corrin.

Sydney shook her head. "You wouldn't believe me if I told you. I barely believe me and I'm living it."

"Try me."

Sydney could only stare at Shawn. She blinked back tears before she turned away to watch Orlaith again.

When Sydney remained quiet, Chelsea spoke. "It happened when we went to the museum. Corrin was a Celtic warrior trapped by a spell that could only be broken by the kiss of a grateful virgin he'd helped. Sydney hid behind him and thought she'd kiss him as a joke and thank him for hiding her. It set Corrin and Orlaith free. And now Sydney and Corrin are bound together until he does her a great service."

Shawn stared at each of them in turn. "I haven't had enough to drink to believe that crap."

Sydney glared at him as she gestured towards the beach. "What do you call her then?"

"Psychotic?"

"But it's true," Chelsea protested.

Sydney made a sharp motion with her hand. "Forget it Chelz. Let him think what he wants. I'm sick of this. It's like having a Siamese freakin twin."

"Why would I believe you? The lot of you sound insane. It's not… hang on. You're a virgin?" Shawn stared at Sydney.

"Let me guess. That's the hardest part for you to believe?" Sydney shook her head in disbelief.

"You're seventeen."

"So?"

"You're not, I don't know," Shawn made a movement with his hand as if to fill in the blank with his motion. "A… a," he shook his head and his expression brightened. "A religious nut. You know, one of those ones who are waiting for marriage."

"No. Now can we just drop the subject?" Sydney glared at Shawn defiantly.

"You must be the last seventeen-year-old virgin." Shawn didn't seem to be in the least bit ready to drop the conversation.

"Not hardly," Chelsea said.

"It's like an epidemic." Shawn looked from Sydney to Chelsea and slowly shook his head.

"Oh shut up." Sydney gestured towards the beach. "What are we going to do about her? I can't spend every night in the ocean." She rubbed her arms. "I'm freezing already."

Shawn grinned. "I'll keep you warm."

Sydney held up a hand. "Don't even think about it."

"We might have to do more than think about it. We are going to get a lot colder as the night ages," Corrin said.

"This is all your fault." Sydney pointed a finger at Corrin. "You said she was a sister to you. What were you doing kissing her?"

"On the cheek. She tells just enough truth to make

her words seem honest. But they are always twisted to serve her purpose," Corrin said.

"So how did you kiss Sydney? Are you going to tell me that was on the cheek too?" Shawn demanded.

Corrin shook his head. "No. That was not at all sisterly."

Shawn took a swing at Corrin who blocked him and twisted his fist behind him. "Do not push me."

"Let him go." Sydney couldn't keep the weariness from her voice. "I just want this all to be over."

The moment he was released, Shawn moved away from Corrin. "Is this why we broke up? Because you're stuck with him?"

"It doesn't matter," Sydney said.

Shawn moved to stand in front of her. "Yeah, it does. I don't want us to be over. And I don't think you do either. Come on Sydney. Don't let this mess ruin everything."

Sydney turned away, looking out to sea. There were lights dotting the horizon and she wondered what type of boats sat out there. "I can't deal with this. I just can't."

"But after?" Shawn rested a hand on her shoulder.

Sydney shrugged it off. "Don't push me."

"Can we forget all the dramas for a minute?"

Chelsea asked through chattering teeth. "I'm going to be an iceblock shortly."

Sydney pushed through the water to reach her friend's side and wrapped her arms around her. "I'm sorry I dragged you into this."

"Maybe I should be making you do a great service for me in payment." Chelsea grinned. "Oh the things I could ask."

Sydney tried to resist, but couldn't help returning Chelsea's grin. "No more thinking. Anyone'd believe you were about to write your letter to Santa. And I'm certainly no Santa Claus."

Chelsea leaned back slightly to look her friend up and down. "Hmm, I don't know. There's a resemblance somewhere, I just can't put my finger on it. Are you putting on weight?"

"Remember I'm the one keeping you warm," Sydney warned.

"You're not doing a very good job of it. I'm still freezing. Isn't summer meant to be on the way?"

Corrin moved to Chelsea's side. "Do you need more warmth?"

"Yep." Chelsea's grin returned. "You can plaster yourself all over me any time you want."

Corrin frowned. "You all have such an odd way

of speaking." He put his arms around Chelsea so that they rested on Sydney's arms.

"You're not leaving me out in the cold." Shawn pressed in close to Sydney, his arms sliding around her waist to rest between her and Chelsea.

Sydney briefly met Corrin's gaze over Chelsea's shoulder before she turned her gaze to the moonlit water. "I always used to wonder what my grandma meant when she said 'no good deed goes unpunished.' I finally know."

"What are we going to do while we wait for dawn?" Chelsea asked.

Shawn's breath brushed the back of Sydney's neck. "I think this is one of those times where more than two is a crowd."

"What I really want right now is a wetsuit." Sydney turned her head to look at Shawn who pressed his lips against her neck. "And if you don't behave I'm going to put my elbow through your ribs."

"You don't really mean that. You're just stressed. We'll sort this problem out and then we'll talk about us. And there'll be no more games," Shawn said.

"There are always games," Corrin said. "Even when people think they are not playing them."

"Stay out of this." Shawn's arms tightened around Sydney.

"I'm not talking about any of this right now." Sydney paused before she met Chelsea's gaze. "I have no idea what we're going to do until dawn. Suggestions would be good."

Chelsea giggled. "Truth or dare certainly wouldn't be the right game for this situation. Wasn't that our standard 'break the boredom' game when we were younger?"

"We are so not going there, okay?" Sydney turned her head to address Shawn. "And will you ease up? I do need to breathe."

Shawn loosened his hold. "I always liked the dares in truth or dare."

"What is this truth or dare?" Corrin asked.

"Forget it," Sydney muttered. "What about word association?"

It took about ten minutes for Corrin to understand the game, but less than an hour later they fell into silence. Other than Orlaith, the beach was empty. Sydney glared at her and wished there was some way they could get rid of her.

Sydney shifted her weight. "I want to sit down."

"You can lean back against me. I'll hold you up," Shawn said.

She hesitated, feeling guilty when she met Corrin's unreadable gaze. After a moment, she leaned back, her head against Shawn's shoulder as she let his arms support her weight. Corrin's gaze remained unreadable. "I wonder how many hours we have left."

Corrin looked upwards. "We are not even half way through the night."

"How do you know?" Shawn asked.

"The position of the moon." Corrin motioned towards it with a nod of his head.

"The moon varies its rise and set times," Shawn said.

"Not that quickly. I check the position every night. It's a habit. And the stars too. They are very different from my time. I sometimes think I recognise a group, but they look strange. Do they have names and stories like the stars from my time did?"

Chelsea lifted her arm to point. "That's the Southern Cross, and there's Orion's Belt. That's the only ones I know. I think there's some story about Orion, but I wouldn't have a clue what it is."

Chapter Eighteen

"Orion was a Greek hunter. If you were from Celtic England then the reason why the stars would only look a little familiar is because we're on the other side of the world to England," Shawn said. "You should be able to find out more on the net."

"Of course he's from Celtic England," Sydney muttered.

"Sydney showed me cars on the net. Do you think they would have one of those documentaries about stars?" Corrin asked.

Shawn shrugged. "I don't know. Probably. But if they don't there's heaps of stuff you could read."

"I cannot read."

"Serious?" Shawn stared at him.

Corrin smiled slightly. "You have the same expression a man from my time would have if someone told him they had no idea how to defend themselves."

Shawn swore. "The sword fighting. That wasn't a game to you. And the scars. They aren't from a car accident, are they?"

Corrin shook his head. "No. They are from battle."

"All of them?"

"Or training." Corrin smiled. "Sometimes there are accidents."

Shawn stared at Corrin. "You weren't lying to me? You really are a Celtic warrior?"

"I'm not lying."

"What's it like?"

"What?"

"War."

Corrin frowned. "It is hard to explain. Noisy. There are battle cries, weapons clashing, screams of wounded horses. Noise. It is what is most noticeable. That and the blood as the day ages. In some battles the ground is soaked with it."

Sydney shuddered. "Let's not talk about blood soaked ground. Not when Orlaith is still pacing the beach with her bow and arrows. And you still haven't told me what we're going to do about her. We can't spend every night in the ocean." Sydney sneezed.

"Great. I better not be coming down with a cold from this."

"What does saltwater do to Orlaith?" Shawn asked.

"Burns. She cannot cross a line of salt either," Corrin said.

"We need water pistols," Shawn said.

Sydney shook her head. "No, we need a soaker. One with a really large water tank."

Chelsea yawned. "If I fall asleep, please don't let me drown."

"You better organise something better for tomorrow night," Sydney warned.

Corrin nodded. "We will buy salt and make a circle around the house. If we bury it a few inches under the ground Orlaith cannot use wind to break through the circle."

"But what if she's in the house when we make the circle?" Sydney asked.

"Does it matter which side of the circle she is on? We can cross it at will," Corrin said.

"I guess." Sydney fell quiet for a few minutes. "How long do you think we've got left until dawn?"

"It is the middle of the night," Corrin said.

Sydney sighed. "I'm going to start wearing a watch. A waterproof one."

Corrin looked at the beach. "Quiet. A group of

people are coming up the beach. Sound travels well over water."

Sydney looked in the direction Corrin watched and enviously stared at the handful of people walking along the beach, laughing, talking and shoving at each other. She closed her eyes. To rest them or to ignore the scene. She didn't know. It seemed like only moments before she was woken by the soft murmur of voices.

"You can't stop me from seeing her." Shawn's voice had an edge of anger to it.

"I will not stand back and watch you hurt her with more of your games," Corrin warned.

"It has nothing to do with you."

"Do you love her?"

There were a few minutes of silence before Shawn spoke. "I care. Who really knows about love at our age?"

"The heart does not care about age," Corrin said.

"Maybe not in your time. Weren't you lot old by thirty?"

"You do not love her."

Shawn's arms tightened momentarily around Sydney. "And I suppose you do."

"We are not discussing my feelings. I will not have you hurt her again."

"She can't have been too hurt if she was kissing you within hours of breaking up with me." The anger in Shawn's voice was joined by bitterness.

"Minutes."

"What?"

"It was within minutes of breaking up with you."

Shawn's body went rigid. "And you pointed that out because?" He sounded like he spoke through clenched teeth.

"Because you did not have your facts correct."

"Am I supposed to thank you," Shawn demanded.

"Shut up," Chelsea grumbled. "I was trying to sleep."

"There is light in the east. The sun will rise soon," Corrin said.

Sydney opened her eyes to find Corrin's gaze on her. His lips momentarily curved into a smile, but his gaze remained on hers. In the end, it was Sydney who turned away to look out across the water as she straightened, pressing her feet against the sand again.

"Good morning," Shawn murmured against her cheek.

"The only good is we're getting out of the water soon." Sydney wriggled her fingers, wincing at the rush of pins and needles. "My fingers are more wrinkled than an old lady's."

"I kind of liked having you sleep all over me." Shawn's words were a whisper against her ear.

Sydney couldn't tell what it was that made her think Corrin had heard. What she could see of his stance? Maybe the tightness of his jaw. Whatever it was, it sent a wave of guilt through her followed by one of anger. She pulled away from Shawn and Chelsea. "I'm going to take a swim." Anything had to be better than worrying that a fight would start.

Chelsea yawned. "It's too early."

"I need to get my circulation going. It'll probably help me warm up. Come on Chelz. It'll do you good."

Chelsea pulled away from Corrin to stretch. "They say that about vegetables, but it doesn't mean I go out of my way to eat them."

Sydney smiled and brushed her hand across the top of the water with enough force to send a light spray towards Chelsea. "Come on." She struck out through the water, the beach to her right, before Chelsea had a chance to retaliate. Within minutes they were all swimming beside her. Once she'd swum a couple of hundred metres she turned and headed back to the point where they'd spent the night. The sun was cresting the horizon as she stopped and looked towards the beach with a frown. "Are we in a different spot?"

"We moved a bit with the tide," Corrin said.

Chelsea swam towards the shore, her head above water as she lazily moved forward. "About time Orlaith left the beach. I hope she had as bad a night as I did."

"It wasn't too bad a night." Shawn's gaze remained on Sydney.

She had no clue what to say. "I need a shower. I feel like my bikini is full of sand and I have a permanent layer of salt on my skin." She dived under the water, arrowing towards the beach. When she surfaced, she ploughed through the water to put distance between her and her problems. Both of them. Her plan failed. They kept pace with her. As she neared the beach, she rose to walk the rest of the way, forcing her legs through the water and cutting through the waves. The sea lapped around her ankles as she stopped to twist water out of her hair, biting back a smile as she saw Chelsea and Corrin do the same.

Shawn ran his hands back from his forehead and down the back of his head to remove the excess water from his hair. "What do we do now?"

"This is not your concern," Corrin said.

"Don't start that crap again. I'm staying." Shawn strode across the beach towards his car.

Corrin was close on his heels. "You broke up. Sydney is nothing to you now."

Chelsea linked her arm through Sydney's. "Some people have all the luck. Where are the gorgeous guys fighting over me? Wanna share?"

Sydney couldn't help laughing. "You can have both of them. I'm likely to drown them if they keep this up." They ambled across the beach to where Corrin and Shawn waited silently by the car.

Shawn leaned on the open driver's door and held out Sydney's clothes and phone to her as she reached him. "Try not to get my car all wet and sandy." He looked at each of them as he spoke, his gaze coming to a rest on Sydney again.

With a nod, Sydney took her gear and headed for the passenger door. She lay her shirt on the seat before she hopped in. She buckled up as the other doors closed and sat in silence as they returned to the house. It appeared the same. They all sat in the car and stared at it, the misty figure of Orlaith leaned against the wall near the front door. She drew back a misty arrow and shot it towards them.

Sydney swung the door open. "She's not welcome

here." She strode across the damp grass. "You hear me, Orlaith? You're not welcome here."

Orlaith smiled. "I go where I please."

Sydney ran a hand through Orlaith as she heard the car doors open and close behind her. "Go away."

Orlaith broke up into mist then reappeared a metre away with a laugh. "Tonight. I am going to enjoy making you pay for that tonight."

"You said you wouldn't kill me," Sydney said.

"You will live." Orlaith paused, a smile curving her lips into an expression of satisfaction. "But you will beg to die." She broke up into mist, her laugh hanging on the air as she vanished.

"What about if we find a salt pan before tonight? Do you think she could cross that?" Chelsea asked.

"What is a salt pan?" Corrin opened the front door and checked the room.

"A large flat ground that is covered in salt and other minerals." Shawn followed Corrin into the house. "They were usually once a lake or part of the sea and have dried up leaving the salt behind."

"Is there one around here?" Corrin asked.

Shawn shrugged. "I wouldn't have a clue. You could probably find out online."

Sydney headed for her room, calling over her shoulder, "I'm first in the shower."

"I'm second." Chelsea went to collect fresh clothes.

Once they had showered, dried their hair with the hair dryer and had breakfast, they dragged the mattresses to the lounge room and dropped onto them. Sydney was more resigned than annoyed to find Corrin on one side of her and Shawn on the other.

Chelsea sent her a grin as she glanced past Shawn who was between them. "Still complaining?"

Sydney laughed. "I'm too tired to care." She dropped back to stare at the ceiling.

"About what?" Shawn turned on his side to face her.

"Forget it," Sydney muttered as she rolled onto her side, her back to him. She closed her eyes when she saw Corrin's smile.

Chapter Nineteen

"Out of bed now!"

Sydney rubbed her eyes as she sat up, blinking as she tried to make sense of her parents standing over her. "Mum? Dad?"

"How are we expected to trust you when you do something like this?" Victoria gestured towards Shawn and Corrin.

With a groan Sydney dropped back on the mattress. "It's not what you think."

"Pack your clothes and get in the car," Malcolm said.

"What? No!" Sydney looked from her parents to Corrin, her brain frantically trying to come up with a plan.

"This is not up for discussion," Victoria said firmly.

"But you don't understand." Sydney struggled to

her feet, taking the hand Corrin held out to her. "Mum-"

"I have been ringing you all morning. How do you think I felt when I couldn't contact either of you girls?" Victoria picked up the phone Sydney had left on the bench after she'd finished in the bathroom. "I can see now why you turned it off and didn't want to be disturbed."

Sydney took her phone and turned it on. "It wasn't deliberate. We were at the beach."

Chelsea grabbed her phone, turned it on and groaned when she saw all the missed calls. "You rang my parents?"

Malcolm pulled out his phone. "Of course we did. And I'm ringing them right now to inform them you're both still alive and not the victim of some serial killer like your mum thought."

Sydney laughed, a sharp mirthless sound. "I wonder if Orlaith counts."

Malcolm finished his phone call and slid his phone in his pocket as he turned to Shawn who stood near Corrin. "Is that your car out the front?"

Shawn nodded. "Yeah."

"I want to talk to you boys. The drive back home will be as good a time as any." Malcolm held out his hand. "The keys."

Shawn glanced towards Sydney who shrugged. He hesitated then handed them over.

Sydney headed for the bedroom to get dressed. Maybe this would work. Two cars, both headed to the same destination. If they left at the same time they shouldn't get too much distance between them. As soon as she dressed, she packed up hers and Corrin's clothes, leaving him out a set for the day. She put Orlaith's arrows, that Corrin had gathered, in with his gear. She paused in the doorway where Corrin waited to enter the bedroom.

"Everything will be okay."

Sydney smiled slightly as he stressed the word okay. "I hope so." She slipped past him to freeze at the look on her mum's face. It didn't look like they were going to have a pleasant trip home.

"Put your gear in the car, girls." Victoria's tone ensured there were no arguments.

Chelsea dropped her bag in the back and turned to Sydney, her voice a low murmur. "What are we going to do?"

Sydney put hers and Corrin's bags in and closed the car. Her skin felt tight already. "Just don't argue with her. That'll make it worse."

"But what about you and Corrin?" Chelsea looked

over to where Corrin and Shawn stood on the short front verandah.

"They'll be following in Shawn's car." Sydney couldn't help resting her gaze on Shawn. "I wonder if that talk will make him head for the hills."

"Were you thinking of getting back with him?"

Sydney shrugged. "I don't know." Her gaze was drawn to Corrin who stood with his arms by his side, his gaze on her. "I don't know anything."

Victoria finished talking to Malcolm and strode towards them. "In the car."

"Isn't Dad leaving now?" Sydney sent a nervous glance towards her dad.

"That doesn't concern you right now. You need to be thinking about the fact you lied to us and have gone behind our backs and that you'll probably be grounded for life." Victoria opened the back door. "Get in Chelsea."

Chelsea hesitated. "What about locking up the house?"

"Mal will do that before they leave. Now you girls need to get in the car. I am fast losing patience."

Chelsea hopped in the car but Sydney hesitated. "When are they leaving?"

"Get in the car, Sydney. Now." Victoria gestured towards the front passenger seat.

"Dad? When are you leaving?" Sydney couldn't keep the worry from her voice.

"As soon as we lock up. Now get in the car, Sydney. You're in enough trouble already," Malcolm said.

Sydney hesitated a moment longer, her gaze meeting Corrin's. His expression was unreadable. Off to the side she saw the misty figure of Orlaith appear, a satisfied smile again on her face before she vanished from sight. She was torn. Refuse to go and get into more trouble? Leave and have her skin feel like it was shrinking? Stay and risk Orlaith harming her parents? She turned her gaze to her mum's throat. It was bare. A glance at her dad showed he wore his amulet. How long could it take him to lock up? Surely not long. She shakily got in the front of the car.

As the car pulled out onto the road, Sydney felt her skin tighten further and turned to look at the house. Corrin and Shawn stood by the car. A headache exploded and Sydney gritted her teeth as she tried to ignore the pain. They turned a corner and the house was lost to view. She pulled out a tissue in time to catch the blood that dripped from her nose.

"Sydney?" Chelsea's gaze and voice were filled with worry.

Sydney couldn't answer. She felt her phone vibrate in her pocket and fished it out to hand it to Chelsea.

Chelsea answered it. "Shawn? You're on speaker."

"What is he ringing for?" Victoria demanded.

"What's going on?" Shawn asked. "Corrin isn't looking good and he's bleeding like someone turned on a tap."

"Haven't you left yet?" Chelsea asked.

"Mal's still locking up. What's going on? And why isn't Sydney answering her phone?" Shawn swore. "He collapsed. Corrin just collapsed. Sydney! Can you hear me? What's happening?"

Sydney tried to reach out to take the phone. Her body wouldn't obey. Her hand fell to her side and she felt blood drip over her lips and onto her chin. The world seemed miles away and she could barely keep her eyes open. Her entire body was filled with pain. She would have screamed if her voice still worked.

"They're dying," Chelsea's voice broke on a sob.

"Don't be so dramatic, Chelsea," Victoria said.

"Look at her. You're killing her."

"Will someone tell me what to do?" Shawn screamed over the phone.

Sydney met her mum's gaze through her own slitted gaze. She saw the look of shock, then felt the car jerk to a sudden stop as Victoria pulled onto the side of the road. Her mum shook her. She watched as blood splashed her mum, who seemed to be speaking without sound. All Sydney could hear was a buzzing noise. She saw Chelsea lean forward, her hands gesturing, her mouth also moving. The car started again, turning back the way it had come. Sydney heard fragments of sentences. Hospital. Dying. Blood. Her eyes finally closed as the pain started to ease. She heard her name called over and over again. But she had no energy to answer.

The moment the car stopped her door was jerked open and Sydney opened her eyes to see Corrin clinging to the door. She stumbled out into his arms, her skin returning to normal as her body pressed against his. They tumbled to the ground and lay on the grassed footpath, arms wrapped around each other. About her she could hear voices yelling. She ignored them.

"I'm sorry," Corrin murmured against her hair.

"I don't want to know how close that was." Sydney shuddered. "We're alive. I can't believe we're alive."

"I did not think we would take so long to leave." Corrin's arms tightened about her.

"Neither did I. We're alive." Her hands slid under the back of Corrin's shirt to press against his warm skin, feeling the ridge of a scar. "I thought-" she broke off, unable to complete that sentence.

Corrin's lips met hers, the arguing still going on around them. "I will not leave it to someone else to keep you safe. No matter who they are."

She tasted blood. A sharp metallic taste. How much had they both lost? She didn't care. They were alive. For now.

"Enough!" Victoria's voice rang out over all the noise bringing silence. "I want to know what is going on. Immediately."

Sydney turned in Corrin's arms so she could see her mum. "Corrin is my Siamese twin and we're still waiting for the surgery to separate us."

Malcolm frowned and gestured towards Shawn. "I thought you were dating him."

"We broke up," Sydney said.

"Then what's he doing here?" Victoria asked.

"He wants me back," Sydney said.

"But you're with Corrin now?" Malcolm asked.

Sydney shook her head. "I told you, we're only Siamese twins. He's not my boyfriend."

"It doesn't look that way to me." Victoria's gaze dropped to Corrin's arms that were still around her.

"Nearly dying tends to freak me out." Sydney struggled to her feet.

Corrin rose and helped her stand. He kept an arm around her waist for support. "I am sorry for the lies. Sydney did not think you would understand."

"So who are you really?" Malcolm asked.

"He's the stone statue of the Celtic warrior that was stolen." Sydney leaned against Corrin, her legs feeling like jelly.

Chapter Twenty

"Try again. This time I want the truth," Victoria said.

"He's a little clueless when it comes to the modern world but he knows all about killing with a sword and Celtic jewellery." Sydney laughed at the flare of interest she saw in her mum's eyes at the mention of jewellery.

"Don't be cruel, Sydney. What's really going on? Is it drugs?" Victoria asked.

Sydney sighed and wiped at her face. "I knew you wouldn't believe me." Her skin felt tight where the blood had dried against it. A different tight to what she felt when Corrin wasn't near her. "I need to use the bathroom." She eyed Corrin. "So do you."

Malcolm looked around. "We should probably take this discussion inside." He turned to Shawn. "But you can go home. This has nothing to do with you and Sydney isn't interested in being your girlfriend."

"I spent an entire night freezing my arse off in the ocean to avoid being ventilated by arrows. I'd say I'm well and truly part of this," Shawn said.

"Arrows! Sydney, what's going on?" Victoria demanded.

Sydney held Corrin's hand and headed for the house. "You haven't believed a single word I've said. I'm wasting my breath."

"Sydney. Get back here now." Victoria pointed to the ground in front of her.

After a glance towards her mum, Sydney kept walking. "I need to use the bathroom." Once the bathroom door was closed, she leaned back against it to stare at Corrin. "You're a mess."

"Look in the mirror. You do not look any better."

Sydney pushed away from the door and grabbed the face washer that hung over the bathtub taps. She rinsed it out and ran it across Corrin's cheek and over his chin. "I'm sorry. I should have ignored them. Or tried harder. Something."

Corrin took the washer from her and rubbed his face. "You did what you thought was best." He turned and rinsed the washer before he gently wiped her face.

"But it wasn't the best. I nearly got us killed." She swayed on her feet, still feeling nauseated. She watched as Corrin rinsed the washer again, the water turning red. "How much blood can you lose before it kills you?"

Corrin turned to her with a grin. "I have lost well more than this during a battle and still walked away."

Sydney shook her head slowly. "That isn't something to be proud of."

"Walking away from battle?"

"No, losing a heap of blood in battle."

Corrin laughed softly. "Maybe not in your world." He ran the washer over her face one more time before he cleaned the streaks of blood from her arms.

Sydney stared up at him. "What are we going to do?" Her words were soft.

"Whatever it takes to survive." He dropped the washer in the sink behind him and slid his arms around her waist. "Next time I will ignore your orders if they put you in danger."

She rested her head against his chest. "I didn't give any orders." They should return to the lounge room, but she needed a few more minutes. She wasn't looking forward to the questions she still had to answer. How could she convince her parents of the truth?

"Your actions were your orders."

"I didn't know what to do. I thought Dad would follow us. I didn't think he'd be that far behind."

There was a loud knock on the bathroom door. "How long do you need?" Victoria demanded.

"I don't want to go out there," Sydney whispered.

Corrin checked the window. "I think the door is the only way to leave the bathroom."

Sydney sighed and slowly pulled away from him. "What am I going to tell them?"

"The truth?"

"Like they're going to believe that." Sydney shrugged. "I guess it'll have to do. It's not like I can think of anything else to say." She hesitated, her hand on the doorknob. "I've got a killer headache."

"Sydney. Hurry up." Victoria's voice was filled with impatience.

"Okay!" Sydney flung the door open. "Give me a break." She felt Corrin at her back, the warmth of him comforting.

"I want an explanation of what's going on. Now." Victoria's hands went to her hips and her eyes narrowed. "And it better be the truth."

Sydney stepped into the room, her gaze flickering to Chelsea and Shawn who both looked uneasy. She took a deep breath, not looking forward to the coming discussion. She turned to her mum. "You have to promise not to interrupt. You need to let me tell you all of it." She faced her dad. "Both of you."

"You can't expect us to stand around listening to lies," Victoria warned.

Sydney met Chelsea's gaze. "Grab Corrin's bag." Then faced her parents again. "Even if you think it's lies, let me tell you everything. Then you can argue all you want." When her parents didn't answer straight away, she added, "Please."

Malcolm nodded first then Victoria spoke. "Then you'll answer all our questions."

Sydney nodded. "Deal." She started the explanation while Chelsea was still outside, coming to an end well after Chelsea had returned and dropped the bag at her feet. As soon as she had finished her explanation, she opened the bag while her parents were still staring at her like she'd gone way past insanity. She withdrew Orlaith's arrows, handed some to her mum and the rest to her dad.

"Where did you get these from?" Victoria looked up from the arrows she'd examined.

"I told you. Orlaith." Sydney waited for more questions. There was silence as her parents shared a look. Her heart sank as she recognised that look.

"Typical of Orlaith not to be around when we need her." Chelsea's gaze searched the room for the mist Orlaith was forced to be during the day. "Psychotic bitch."

"Chelsea." There was a reprimand in Victoria's tone.

"Well she is." Chelsea crossed her arms over her chest. "She tried to kill me."

"She tried to kill all of us," Shawn said.

Chelsea shook her head. "Not Sydney. She doesn't want to risk breaking the bond."

The misty form of Orlaith appeared beside Malcolm causing him to jump back. "I don't want to kill Corrin either." She slowly crossed the room to trail a misty finger across his shoulder as she walked behind him. She paused at the opposite shoulder. "I want to make him suffer." She laughed as she strode away from him to stand in front of Victoria. "Someone who doesn't believe. How… lovely." She rushed at Victoria, seeming to fade into her.

Victoria shuddered.

Malcolm ran to his wife, grabbing her by the shoulders. "Victoria? Are you okay? Did she do something to you?"

Corrin picked up the saltshaker that was sitting on the kitchen bench near him and unscrewed the lid. He strode towards Victoria, tipping a white mound into his hand, throwing it at her.

Victoria raised her hands as the salt came towards her and Malcolm turned on Corrin. Before he could speak, Victoria gasped, and seemed to smoke. Orlaith formed in the air in front of Victoria who fell to her knees, her arms wrapped around her waist as Malcolm joined her on the ground.

"Are you okay? What happened? Vic?"

Victoria could only shake her head as Orlaith screamed curses at Corrin.

Chelsea held onto her amulet and Shawn stepped to her side. "I need one of those." He pointed to the amulet. "No way do I want her in my body."

"You can't hurt my parents." Sydney glared at Orlaith. "Just like Chelsea. It'd be a great service if Corrin had to save them from you."

Orlaith laughed. "I did not hurt her. I was only playing. Such a pretty little poppet." She pouted. "You do not want me to have any fun." She came close enough to Sydney to pat her on the cheek.

Sydney stepped back from the cold, misty fingers. "Leave me alone."

"Show a little gratitude. I did you a favour."

Sydney stared at Orlaith. "Favour! Taking over my mum's body wasn't a favour."

Orlaith smiled. "No. Convincing your parents of

your truth was the favour. So what will you do for me in return? You do not want to owe me."

Corrin joined Sydney, the shaker in one hand, a fist full of salt in the other. "We owe you nothing. You only appeared for your own gain. I don't know what that is but I know you well enough to be certain it was for your benefit."

"Darling brother, you wound me." Orlaith pressed her hand to her heart. "How could you think so badly of me? And after all we have meant to each other."

Corrin's hand reached for a sword that was no longer at his side. "The only favour I owe you is death for what you have done to me. And for the pain you caused Lorcan."

Orlaith laughed. "You have to catch me first. And you are not clever enough for that." She rushed at him, disappearing before she came into contact with the salt.

Shawn reached Corrin's side and took the saltshaker. "This is mine until someone gets me an amulet."

"I'll make one later. I still have some gold left over from the armband I melted," Corrin said.

Victoria struggled to her feet, with Malcolm's help. "I told you some of the clay was missing."

"Forget the clay. He melted down one of his armbands," Malcolm said. "What a waste."

"Do you have more?" Victoria turned to Corrin.

Sydney slowly shook her head. "I should have known. Don't worry, Mum. There's still plenty left. He has a bag full of jewellery."

"Where is it?" Victoria asked.

"In my room."

"You left it lying around? Anyone could steal it." Victoria sounded appalled.

"It's not exactly lying around. It's in my wardrobe."

Victoria stared at her. "Don't you understand the value of it? You should have put it in our safe."

"Seriously? And how would I have explained it? Mum! Look at you. You've spent most of the day telling me I'm lying."

"Well you have to admit it's a bit hard to swallow," Malcolm said.

"Exactly. So how could I tell you? And I really don't think I should be grounded either. It's not fair. It's not like you would have believed me," Sydney said.

"But you were going to sneak off and visit Shawn." Malcolm glanced towards him as he said his name.

"But I didn't," Sydney argued.

"I think it's fair to ground you until the end of the holidays," Victoria said.

"What!" Sydney looked from one parent to the other. "No! That's not fair."

"Nor is getting yourself into this much danger," Malcolm said.

"What about my parents?" Chelsea asked. "Are you going to tell them?"

Malcolm and Victoria shared a look until Victoria shook her head. She turned to Chelsea. "No. There's no way we can get them to understand this."

"She can't stay on her own. Orlaith will kill her." Sydney reached out to wrap an arm around Chelsea's waist. "I won't let that happen."

Chapter Twenty-One

Malcolm ran his hands through his hair. "I'll tell them it was a misunderstanding. You can stay at our place."

"But we're fine here," Sydney protested.

"No you're not. You spent the night in the ocean. It's a wonder you're not all sick," Malcolm said.

Victoria started to pace. "We'll do that salt circle around our house that you said Corrin suggested. I hope it doesn't kill the grass."

"We need to finish tidying up here." Malcolm pointed to the hole in the back of the front door. "And make some repairs."

"Shawn can stay and help you so he can give you a lift back," Victoria said.

"I'm not going home. I'm not letting that psychotic bitch get me," Shawn said. "And I'm not staying here without an amulet."

"You can't expect us to let you stay at our home," Victoria said.

Sydney spoke up before anyone else could. "All of us. I'm not losing anyone to her." When her parents didn't answer, Sydney's expression became determined. "All of us. Or we find somewhere else to stay until we get rid of Orlaith."

"Get rid of me!" Orlaith reappeared, sitting on the kitchen bench. "None of you are clever enough." She held her hand out to admire the back of it. "And look at this. More solid already." She laughed. "I'll be able to walk the earth day and night soon."

Sydney gestured towards Orlaith with her middle finger.

"Sydney!"

Sydney grinned at her mum. "I bet you can't say you weren't tempted to do the same." She made a brushing away motion with her hand. "Forget it. Forget her. What's your answer, Mum?"

Victoria finally answered. "You will all stay in the rumpus room. On separate mattresses."

Sydney stepped forward to throw her arms around her mum. "Thank you."

"And what about an amulet for me?" Shawn asked again.

Sydney drew away from her mum and started to remove her amulet.

Corrin reached out to stop her with a hand on her wrist. He shook his head and removed his own amulet. He turned to throw it towards Shawn. "As long as you keep it on she cannot inhabit your body. But she can still harm you once night falls."

Orlaith slid off the bench. "I did not know you were so keen to have me possess you, Corrin." She stalked towards him.

Corrin smiled slightly, his gaze remaining on Orlaith. "Get me the sunscreen, Sydney." He took the saltshaker back from Shawn as Orlaith stopped in front of him.

Sydney dashed into the bathroom and grabbed the sunscreen off the bathroom vanity. Once she was in the living room, she put some in the hand Corrin held out. "What are you going to do?"

Corrin sprinkled half the salt onto the sunscreen. "Hold out your hand." He tipped the rest of the salt into her hand then mixed the salt and sunscreen mixture and started to apply it to his arms, face and top of his chest. "You can try if you would like, Orlaith."

Orlaith moved close to Corrin, until there were only centimetres between them. "You will not always be protected by salt. I am patient. You should know that very well. Beware. The day will come when you will regret messing with my plans."

"That I will not regret, but the day I regret having known you has long since passed."

"No. Not yet. But you will soon know the meaning of regret and I will enjoy every single moment of it," Orlaith said.

Sydney stared at the salt in her hand. "We'll see who is the one with regrets." She blew gently against the salt, smiling as some of it dusted Orlaith who vanished with a screech of rage and pain. Her smile turned into a grin.

Corrin held out his hands. "More sunscreen and the rest of the salt."

She tipped the rest of the salt into Corrin's outstretched hand and added some sunscreen. She watched as he applied the rest of the mixture to the exposed parts of his flesh. She dragged her gaze away from him. "Let's get ready for tonight. There's no way I'm spending another night in the ocean."

Within ten minutes, Victoria was again driving towards home. This time Corrin was in the car. Chelsea sat in the front while Sydney leaned her head against Corrin's shoulder in the backseat. She closed her eyes, still tired after her exhausting night.

They stopped at a swimming pool shop on the way home to buy several bags of pool salt. The rest of the day was spent digging a shallow circle around the house to bury the line of salt. It was late afternoon when there was only a small channel left to fill with salt. They all stood around waiting for Corrin to fill it in, including Malcolm and Shawn who had returned several hours ago.

"Hurry up." Chelsea glanced at the sky. "What are you waiting for? Dark?"

Corrin shook his head. "Move back." He stepped away from the channel. "Orlaith. You might want to come and talk to us." He was greeted by silence. "I will only make this offer once. You cannot stop us from creating a circle of safety. But it will be up to you which side of it you are on. You can stay near the house and have only a small area to roam tonight. Or you can leave through this gap and have the rest of the earth to roam. Whichever you choose you cannot get near us. We can step in and out of the circle."

Orlaith appeared beside him. "You think you are clever. This will not end things. There will come a time when I am as human as you and nothing," she gestured towards the open channel. "Not even your pathetic little tricks will stop me."

"You have to the count of five to make your choice," Corrin said.

"I will remember this. Every thing you do against me you will pay in pain and blood." Orlaith glanced towards Sydney. "And so will she." Orlaith stepped out of the circle. "Sleep in your beds this night. They will not be a haven forever." She turned her back on them and walked away, vanishing.

Corrin tipped salt into the channel and covered it over. He straightened up and dusted his hands on the back of his jeans. "Time to make another amulet."

Victoria involuntarily touched the amulet hanging at her throat. "I've been waiting to see you do that."

"And the jewellery," Malcolm said.

Sydney rolled her eyes. "How considerate of me that I brought back a warrior whose father happened to be a craftsman."

Victoria grinned. "Should we consider this an early Christmas present?"

Sydney reluctantly smiled. "I said you'd want to adopt him."

"It isn't like he has anyone in this century," Victoria pointed out.

"You can't keep him. He's not a pet," Sydney protested.

Malcolm laughed. "We know that." He messed

Sydney's hair and she glared at him as she tidied it. "It's just that there's a market for replica Celtic jewellery and here we have a kid who knows more about it than anyone else alive."

"You pair are unbelievable," Sydney muttered as they stepped inside the front door. Sending a longing glance towards her room, she sighed. This wasn't the time to be holed up in her room. She had to follow her Siamese twin.

Before Sydney could follow Corrin into the workroom, Victoria drew her aside. She waved everyone else forward. "How far can you be from him?"

Sydney shrugged. "Not far. Even at this distance I can feel it."

"How about the kitchen?"

Sydney's eyes narrowed. "Are you asking me to cook dinner?"

"No. I wanted to talk to you. Privately. But if you can, dinner would be good."

Sydney strode to the kitchen, rubbing at her arms. She sat on one of the stools at the island bench. "This is as far as I'm going. Someone else will have to cook."

Victoria nodded as she sat near Sydney.

When her mum remained silent, Sydney smiled. "This isn't another one of those sex talks is it?"

"No. Well sort of. You do realise in his world Corrin would be an adult. Not a young adult either. A man of property. Thinking of children to inherit and hold all he has gained."

"What are you getting at, Mum?"

"I don't want you hurt. And I also don't want you getting into a relationship you're too young to cope with."

"All I'm worried about right now is staying alive."

"That worries me too. You're our baby. You're our responsibility. Not his. It's our job to protect you."

Sydney stared at her mum, trying to think of a tactful way to say the words she was thinking. She failed. "You can't."

Victoria reached out and took her hand. "Sydney–"

"You can't. Corrin is the only one who knows anything about this. She's part of his world."

"I don't know that I can trust him to protect you the way we would."

"Does he look suicidal?"

"What?" Victoria looked startled.

Sydney smiled slightly. "If I die, so does he. Does he look suicidal?"

Victoria shook her head. "Is there anything else you've left out of your tale?"

Sydney shrugged. "I don't know. There was a lot

to remember. And I was trying to keep to the basics since I didn't think you'd listen for long."

"I feel like I'm in a nightmare."

Sydney grinned. "Want me to pinch you?"

Victoria shook her head, an answering grin forming. "Not if you value your life."

Sydney couldn't help laughing. "That's okay. Corrin will protect me."

Victoria sobered. "All those scars…" she faltered.

"In his time he was known as Corrin Harbinger of Death."

"And you wonder why I worry for you."

"That's part of why I don't worry. He will protect me."

"What happens if he dies?"

Sydney didn't want to answer that question. She looked away. She didn't even want to think about the answer. Not after the morning she'd had.

Chapter Twenty-Two

"I guess I have my answer." Victoria wrapped her arms around Sydney, giving her an awkward cuddle as they perched on the stools. "You do know we love you, don't you?"

Sydney nodded.

"And that's why you're grounded."

"That's still not fair," Sydney muttered.

Victoria pulled away with a smile. "Not that it's much of a grounding. You've got three people sleeping over. Your best friend, your ex boyfriend and a man I wouldn't let you date in my worst nightmare. He's a killer, Sydney."

She shook her head. "No. He's a warrior, Mum. A soldier. It's different."

Victoria sighed. "I'm still not going to let you date him. And once you're no longer bound you'll be in separate rooms. And he's out of here as soon as Orlaith is gone."

"Where's he meant to go? He hasn't got anyone but me."

"We'll think of something." Victoria patted her hand. "But I am serious about you not dating him. Look what happened when you tried to go behind our backs and see Shawn."

Sydney drew her hand away from her mum's and rose from the bench. "I knew you'd say that. All this isn't my fault. Orlaith started this centuries ago."

"You didn't need to become a part of it."

Sydney's hands curled into fists. "That isn't fair. Anyway. You should be happy. I brought you home someone who knows how to make jewellery. And design it." Sydney strode to the workroom, ignoring her mum as she called after her. Corrin looked up as she entered the room, pausing in his work. She smiled weakly when Corrin started to move towards her and shook her head. Corrin returned to his work and Sydney retreated to her mum's thinking chair.

Pulling out her phone, Sydney checked her emails, ignoring her mum when she entered the room. Once her emails had been read and replied to she returned her phone to her pocket. She looked over to Corrin who was patiently answering a question her dad had asked. Her gaze dropped to his hands as they worked on the amulet. The same hands she'd seen wield a sword. The hands she knew had earned him the title Harbinger of Death. Her mum wasn't right. He wasn't a killer. He was a soldier. It was different. It wasn't like he went around murdering people in their sleep. It had been war.

At the other end of the table Victoria reverently went through the jewellery she'd taken from Sydney's bedroom. Sydney smiled as she wondered if they were the spoils of war. She was tempted to ask but yawned instead as she wriggled into a more comfortable position. It felt like she'd no sooner drifted off to sleep when Corrin woke her. She blinked up at him, trying to figure out what he'd just said.

"Dinner."

"I'm not up to eggs and toast." Sydney struggled to sit up.

"Chelsea and Shawn cooked. Steak and vegetables Victoria called it."

Sydney checked the room behind him. "Where is everyone?"

"At the dinner table."

"Mum said you're too old for me."

Corrin grinned. "Find out a person is a few

centuries old and suddenly they're not good enough for your daughter."

"It's more than a few centuries. And that wasn't what they meant. They were talking experience and culture."

Corrin's grin remained in place. "If it is just experience you are lacking." He slid his arms around her and pulled her forward. His lips were almost against hers. "I can help with that problem."

Sydney smiled. "Really?" Her tone was dry.

"That word sounds like a challenge."

"What if it is?"

He lightly brushed his lips over hers. "I have a weakness for challenges." His lips returned to hers, this time deepening the kiss.

Sydney lost track of time. She was pulled back to reality by her name being called. She looked towards the doorway where Shawn stood, biting back the urge to apologise. They weren't together. What she did had nothing to do with him. But still she pressed a hand against Corrin's chest to push him away. He rose to his feet and held out a hand to her. Sydney took his hand and reluctantly rose to her feet, walking towards the doorway. Shawn didn't move out of her way.

"I don't care what your parents say. I still want you back."

Sydney met his gaze for a moment before she nodded. "I know you think you do-"

"Sydney-"

She pressed her fingers to his lips. "Let me speak." She quickly moved her fingers when he kissed them and grinned at her. "Don't pressure me. I've got enough to deal with."

Shawn glanced behind her shoulder to Corrin. "Is that what you're calling it these days? What's going on, Sydney?"

"I don't know."

"Is there a chance for us?"

Sydney was conscious of Corrin standing behind her. "I didn't like the games, Shawn. They made me feel like crap."

"I've already promised you there'd be no more games."

She hesitated, searching for the right words. "I don't want to be one of those girls who keeps taking her boyfriend back when he says he won't do it again."

"I wasn't really playing games. I didn't want to smother you or be too possessive." Shawn's gaze flickered to Corrin before returning to Sydney.

"Giving me one chance won't make you weak. Everyone makes mistakes. Come on Sydney, one chance." He reached for her hand.

Victoria entered the corridor behind Shawn. "This reminds me of the toilet roll joke."

Shawn turned towards her with a frown. "The what?"

Victoria looked pointedly at Sydney's hand in Shawn's as she waited for him to let go before she spoke. "How many males does it take to change an empty toilet roll?"

Shawn shrugged. "I don't know."

"Neither does anybody else. It has never happened." Victoria looked at each of them for several seconds. "Did you both forget the reason you offered to fetch Sydney? Dinner is out. And getting cold."

"I'm not hungry. I still feel sick from earlier," Sydney said.

"Since you were able to break the spell keeping Corrin a stone statue, I at least don't have to worry about it being morning sickness," Victoria said.

Sydney rolled her eyes. "Why is everyone so focused on the part about a virgin being needed to break the spell?"

"I wouldn't say focused." Victoria returned along the hallway. She glanced over her shoulder. "I believe the word that comes to mind is relieved. Now hurry up. Dinner. And you can at least have a couple of mouthfuls."

Sydney closed her eyes. "I am so tempted to leave home."

"You can move in with me," Shawn said.

Sydney opened her eyes to glare at him. "No pressure."

Shawn raised his hands in surrender. "I was just offering." He turned and headed for the dining table.

Sydney started to follow, but was stopped by Corrin. She stared down at his hand on her wrist. "What?"

"Are you considering going back to him?"

She continued to stare at his fingers where they encircled her wrist. There was no answer there. "I don't know."

"Sydney–"

She pulled away from him. "Forget it. It's time for dinner."

After an awkward meal and a list of rules, Sydney's parents retired for the night. Once the kitchen was cleaned up, the four of them retreated to the rumpus room so they could discuss their next step. An hour into the discussion, they seemed to be getting nowhere.

Sydney stared at Chelsea who sat opposite her on the mattresses they had pushed together, breaking their first rule for the evening. Corrin and Shawn sat one on either side of her on the same mattress, breaking a second rule.

"This is getting us nowhere." She leaned against Corrin.

Shawn met Sydney's gaze as he gestured towards Corrin. "Is that it? Is that your choice?"

"Quit pressuring me," Sydney snapped. "It's automatic. The closer I am to him the less painful it is. Skin contact causes no pain at all." She frowned. "Actually, it's more like a reversal of pain."

"Reversal or opposite?" Shawn asked. "Because the opposite is pleasure."

Sydney breathed in deeply and heavily, letting it out in a rush. "Reversal. Now shut up and help me figure this out. I want Orlaith dealt with. Before school starts."

"Barely more than a week. That doesn't give us much time." Chelsea held up a hand as if to protect herself when Sydney glared at her. "Don't shoot the messenger."

"Sorry," Sydney muttered as she dropped her head to Corrin's shoulder. "Maybe it's me that should be shot."

Corrin slid his arm around her waist. "I will not let her get to you. Or those you care for. Everyone will be safe."

"I feel like we're going around in circles," Sydney said.

"We all need sleep," Shawn said. "We'll be able to think clearer in the morning."

"I hope so." Sydney continued to rest her head on Corrin's shoulder and closed her eyes.

"Are we going to put the mattresses back to how your mum had them?" Chelsea asked.

Sydney forced her eyes open. "Maybe." She glanced around the room, remembering how much space had been between her and Corrin. "Maybe not." She frowned. "No. Definitely not. I want a decent sleep."

Chapter Twenty-Three

Sydney was dragged from a deep sleep by the murmur of voices. Corrin's arms pulled away from her. With her eyes still closed she captured one arm and drew it back around her. "No more pain. Please. Just let me sleep."

Corrin pressed in close to her again. "Shh. Go back to sleep. I'm not going anywhere."

Sydney tried to open her eyes, but failed. She snuggled against Corrin. "Good. I don't want my body to implode."

"Shh."

She drifted off to sleep again not waking until she smelt toast cooking. Raising her head, she found only Corrin and herself lay on the mattress. He had his back pressed against her as he lay on his side watching her laptop with headphones.

Pausing the program, Corrin removed the

headphones and turned towards her. "Do you feel any better?"

"What do you mean?"

"Every time I moved away you complained it hurt and pulled me back."

Sydney rolled away to the next mattress, stopping once she again faced Corrin. She frowned and with a groan rolled onto her back, her arm falling across her eyes.

Corrin leaned over her. "It is worse, isn't it?"

"I don't need a Siamese twin."

"We are not that close. Shawn showed me what they looked like on the net." Corrin grinned. "Among other things."

Sydney shifted her arm so she could see Corrin's expression better. "Tell me he didn't show you porn." There was a laugh from behind her and Sydney turned her head so she could glare at Shawn.

Shawn's grin matched Corrin's. "You were limiting his education." He took a bite of his half eaten piece of toast, thickly spread with honey.

"And what were you doing? Corrupting his education?" Sydney shifted away from Corrin so she could sit up.

Shawn shook his head. "Not me. Someone else or should I say many someone elses have already done that job. The only thing he learned from the net was about condoms. And I reckon he should seriously think about being tested for STD's, because unlike condom's, they aren't a new invention."

Sydney held up a hand. "I am so not having this conversation." When Shawn opened his mouth to speak again, Sydney interrupted. "Not another word." She rose to her feet, her skin already starting to tighten. "What time is it? Have my parents left for work yet?"

Shawn nodded, his mouth full.

"And they didn't make us separate the mattresses?"

Corrin stood beside her and rested a hand on her shoulder. "I think they were concerned when they heard you moaning about pain every time I moved away from you."

Sydney leaned back against Corrin. "This is impossible. Why is it getting worse?"

"I do not know."

"We have to do something. Anything." Sydney faced Corrin. "Now."

"Shawn talked to a friend of his while you were asleep."

Sydney turned to Shawn. "How will that help?"

"He's doing an advanced certificate in parapsychology."

Sydney felt a moment of empathy for Corrin. "What does that mean in English?"

"He's studying paranormal manifestations and occurrences." When Sydney continued to look blank, Shawn said, "Ghosts and psychics."

"Can he help?"

Shawn shrugged. "I don't know. But he's interested."

"When can we see him?"

"When you're ready," Shawn said.

"Give me half an hour." Sydney started to leave the rumpus room. Feeling the tightening of her skin, she turned and grabbed Corrin's hand, tugging him along with her to her bedroom. As she passed the kitchen, she said good morning to Chelsea who was making toast. In her room she gathered a change of clothes and made Corrin wait at the bathroom door while she quickly dressed. In less than half an hour she was in the backseat of Shawn's car two pieces of toast in one hand and texting a message to her parents with the other.

Sydney smiled when she read her mum's reply. *Be careful. What kind of person studies that?* She tucked her phone into a pocket of her jeans and continued to eat her toast. The drive took a lot longer than she expected and they ended up in an industrial area of town. Shawn's friend lived in a shed with a small area at the back turned into a living area. The front was filled with computers and laptops, in various states of repair, spread out on four large folding tables.

"Come in, come in." He held out a hand to Corrin, then grimaced at the notes scribbled all over his hand in pen. Withdrawing his hand before Corrin had a chance to shake it, he rubbed it against the side of his faded baggy jeans. "It's a bad habit." He gestured towards the fold out chairs at a small table. "Have a seat." Several mugs and coffee stains decorated the top. Theodore folded his lanky frame into one of the chairs and hunched over the table, brushing his dark hair out of his eyes. "Shawn tells me you have a problem with a ghost."

Shawn pointed to each in turn. "This is Sydney, Chelsea and Corrin. Everyone, this is Ted."

Theodore winced at the shortening of his name. "Yes well, your ghost. Shawn tells me she can manifest a real bow and arrows."

"I don't know that I'd call it manifesting. It's like she's alive once it's dark," Sydney said.

"Impossible. Ghosts don't have the power to affect the world around them in more than a rudimentary fashion. Things like slamming doors. Moving light objects, basic things," Theodore said.

"I don't think he's going to be able to help us," Chelsea said. "He doesn't know anything about Orlaith."

"She told you her name?" Theodore pulled a pen from behind his ear and searched for a piece of paper. Giving up, he drew on his wrist. "Or-la. How do you spell that?"

Sydney turned to Shawn. "What did you tell him?"

"The basics."

"Like what? Basically nothing?" Sydney demanded.

Shawn shrugged. "A little more than that. I didn't want to freak him out. We need help, Sydney."

Sydney turned to Theodore. "Orlaith isn't your normal ghost." She paused and frowned. "If there is such a thing as a normal ghost." She waved that question away. "Anyway, she's more of an evil spirit and she has a grudge against Corrin and wants to see him suffer." Sydney glanced around the room. "Actually, she probably wants us all to suffer."

"You need to find out what she wants so you can lay her to rest," Theodore said.

Orlaith appeared by the door, tapping her bottom lip with the tip of one of her arrows. "You have no idea what you are talking about. Sydney told you exactly what I want and you ignored her. Maybe you would like me to add you to the list of those I will make suffer."

Theodore stumbled to his feet, his folding chair collapsing in on itself to land flat on the floor. "She's here. Oh my, oh, oh my goodness. A live ghost." He shook his head. "A dead ghost?" He turned to Corrin. "What did you do to her?"

"Got her killed."

"Oh dear." Theodore checked behind his ear for his pen then realised he'd left it on the table. "Oh dear. I think this is going to be a very difficult puzzle to solve." He scribbled on his arm then examined Orlaith carefully. "She's very beautiful, isn't she?"

Orlaith tapped her arrow against her palm. "He is very dumb, isn't he? It makes me want to rip his brain out since it is obviously of no use to him." She stalked towards Theodore once again tapping the arrow against her lip. "Hmm, where shall I access it from? Through the eyes? The ears? No, an arrow right through the middle of the forehead sounds like a lot more fun." She smiled as if already contemplating her enjoyment.

"Oh dear," Theodore squeaked as he backed away from her.

Corrin held out a spare amulet. "Wear this. You would not want her to possess you."

Theodore grabbed the amulet and slipped it over his head. "Does this work for all manifestations?"

Corrin shook his head. "This has been made to protect against Orlaith."

Shawn sighed. "You know I think you're right. He's not going to be able to help us."

"No, oh no. I will. I'm sure I will. It just wasn't what I was expecting." Theodore gestured towards Orlaith. "I didn't think you'd be bringing her with you."

"We didn't exactly plan to, but she has a mind of her own," Shawn said. "So, how can you help us, Ted?"

Theodore finally found a piece of A4 paper that had been ripped in half. He picked up his chair, unfolded it and sat again. "Maybe you should tell me more than the basics."

Sydney began the story, avoided the part where the spell had to be broken by a virgin then sent Shawn a daggered look when he added in the fact.

"It might be important," Shawn said.

"I don't see how," Sydney muttered before she continued with the story. By the time she'd reached the end, with only a few additions from the others, she was beginning to grow weary of having to retell the story.

When Theodore continued to scribble notes on the crowded piece of paper, Shawn asked, "What do you think, Ted? Are you going to go out there and make us one of those machines that suck up ghosts like they had on Ghostbusters?"

Theodore glanced up from his notes. "That was a movie, Shawn."

Shawn rolled his eyes. "I know that. But we do have a ghost pacing your living room."

"I would not be reduced to pacing if you were more interesting," Orlaith said.

Shawn looked towards Orlaith. "We might invite you to do something fun if you weren't such a psychotic bitch."

Chapter Twenty-Four

Orlaith stopped her pacing to stare at Shawn. "Wait until tonight. When I am finished with you Sydney will not be the only one who rejects you. No one will want you once I have carved you up." She pulled a sharp knife from the sheath attached to her belt. "I do not find it as satisfying as an arrow, but for you I will make an exception."

"She's very blood thirsty, isn't she," Theodore said.

"I wouldn't want you to feel left out. I can carve you up too, if you want." Orlaith played with the tip of her blade. "I am very good at it." She smiled.

"Ur, no, no. I am fine. Thank you. It was kind of you to offer." Theodore's words tumbled out over each other.

"Kind?" Orlaith laughed. "Kind! How entertaining. You I might keep for a pet."

"Ahh, thoughtful of you I'm sure." Theodore

dropped his pen, bent to pick it up and hit his head on the table causing the mugs to rattle. "Now, ah, to the matter at hand. Is there something a little less, ahh, drastic you'd settle for instead of seeing these people suffer?"

"No." Orlaith didn't hesitate.

"Maybe you could come to some kind of understanding-" Theodore began.

Orlaith put her face directly in front of Theodore's. "No. Do you need me to say it again? No. Are you still having trouble understanding? No. No. No. Pain, suffering and a lot of blood and then I will be slightly satisfied."

Theodore leaned as far back as his chair would allow him. "Ahh, good of you to, ahh, clarify that."

Sydney ran her hand through Orlaith forcing her to become mist and reappear back near the door, to glare at them. Sydney ignored her and turned to Theodore. "You might want to stay in a circle of salt once it gets dark. She can't cross it, but her arrows can."

Theodore picked up his pen, his fingers slightly shaking as he made more notes. "Yes, of course. Safe, secure place after dark."

"Can we get back to the reason we're here?" Shawn

glanced towards Orlaith. "What can we do to get rid of her?"

"I don't think-" Theodore began.

"That is right. You don't, do you?" Orlaith interrupted.

"Well, I…" Theodore glanced towards Orlaith. "That is, well-"

"This is a waste of time," Sydney muttered. "We might as well go home and wait for night to arrive."

"Have you considered that, ahh, you should not discuss your, ahh, plans in front of her?" Theodore sent a quick look towards Orlaith.

Shawn rose to his feet. "You're right. You've got my number. Give us a call if you can think of anything. We need to get moving before it's dark." He checked his phone. "It's a lot later than we planned on leaving."

Theodore walked them to Shawn's car, nervous glances towards Orlaith the entire time. He promised to look into the matter and scurried back inside before they got into the car.

"That was a waste of time." Sydney leaned her head against Corrin's shoulder, her hand resting on his jean clad thigh.

Chelsea turned in the front passenger seat to face

Sydney. "We don't know that. He might come up with an idea."

Sydney didn't hold much hope. She turned her attention to the road ahead of them just in time to see Orlaith enter the body of a homeless woman who was pushing a shopping trolley. "Look out!" She leaned forward, pointing.

It was too late. With a very Orlaith like grin, the homeless woman pushed the trolley hard in front of the car. Shawn swore as he collided with the trolley. The car swerved as the front tire blew out and Shawn brought it to a stop in a parking bay.

"We have to get out of here." Sydney checked the area, spotting an empty building site nearby. The homeless woman sat on the footpath, looking dazed, while Orlaith's laughter rang out in the air. Shadows filled the street as the sun reached the horizon.

"We've got to change the tyre," Shawn said.

Sydney shook her head with a look towards the sky. "We don't have time. And who knows who Orlaith will inhabit next." She gestured towards two men far ahead of them on the footpath. Neither had glanced in their direction, even when they'd hit the trolley. "Sunday only means there are no workers about."

Orlaith appeared in front of them. "I warned you. I

don't have to wait till dark. Each of you will pay." She pointed towards Shawn. "You first. Then I go back for your friend."

Chelsea grabbed Sydney's hand. "Come on. We have to find somewhere safe." She tugged Sydney towards the building site, Corrin following.

Orlaith strode down the footpath towards the men. "Running will not help."

"Come on, Shawn." Sydney stopped in front of the chain link fence.

"My car-"

"Forget it. We have to move. She's nearly reached the men." Sydney started to scale the fence, Corrin on one side of her, Chelsea on the other.

"She is playing with us. Like a cat with a mouse." Corrin swung over the top of the fence and dropped to the ground on the other side. "She could have reached us already."

Shawn hesitated a moment longer. He looked between his car and Orlaith. Then, with a quick nod, he scrambled over the fence and they all ran towards the scaffolding that rose against the side of the half finished building.

"We have to hide," Chelsea said.

Sydney headed up the scaffolding. "We need to separate. We can't all stay together."

"No!" Chelsea grabbed Sydney's shoulder as they stopped on one of the platforms. "I'm not going in there alone." She pointed into the dim interior of the building. "You won't be alone. You'll have Corrin with you."

"Then you and Shawn stay together. It'll be impossible for us to find somewhere large enough for all of us to hide." Sydney stepped through a glassless window into the building.

"Sydney–" Chelsea began.

Shawn interrupted. "She's right. We have to hide. Come on." He took Chelsea's hand. "We'll go up another level."

Sydney nodded and headed deeper into the building. She shivered when she heard Orlaith's laughter ring out around her. Was she alone? Or had she found a body to wear?

"Here." Corrin pushed Sydney into an area at the edge of an open wall, scaffolding on one side that led to a long drop. Beyond the drop was another section of the building, mostly metal frames and some flooring. Beside them a pile of timber helped create a hiding place. Corrin put himself between Sydney and the drop.

"Where is she?" Sydney whispered against his ear.

Corrin pressed his finger against her lips, the light slowly fading around them.

Orlaith's voice rang out through the building. "You cannot hide forever. I will find you and for every minute you have made me search I will spill another drop of blood." Footsteps rang out on the concrete floors, heavier than what a slim female would make.

Sydney closed her eyes as she pressed against Corrin's back, his warmth comforting. "Where is she?"

Corrin pointed upwards and Sydney's gaze followed. When she started to open her mouth, he shook his head and again pressed his finger against her lips. Annoyed, Sydney bit his finger. Her annoyance rose when his only response was a grin while he ran his finger across her bottom lip. She pushed him away from her, ignoring his amusement.

"Chelsea! Run!" Shawn's voice sounded above them and Sydney tried to rise from her hiding place.

Corrin pushed her back. "Stay."

Sydney shook her head, pushing against his immovable body. "I have to help Chelsea. Please." Her gaze was drawn to the ceiling where she heard the sound of running. "Please."

There was a scream, then Chelsea called Shawn's

name. Sydney screamed with her when she saw Shawn fall over the edge of the building, his flailing hands grabbing a length of rope that had fallen with him, catching on the scaffolding.

"He's going to cut the rope. He has a knife. Orlaith's making him cut the rope." Chelsea's voice rose higher with each word.

"Corrin. He'll die." Sydney continued to push against him.

Corrin grabbed her hands. "Stay here."

"I can't. We can't be separated."

"Stay here or I do nothing."

Sydney looked past Corrin to where Shawn struggled to reach the floor above him, while Chelsea's warnings filled the air. Her gaze collided with Corrin's. "Save him. Please."

With a single sharp nod, Corrin rose to his feet and ran towards the edge of the building. "Shawn! Let go!" Corrin tackled Shawn in mid air.

Sydney felt her skin tighten to an unbearable level and automatically rose to her feet, moving forward to lessen the pain. The force of Corrin's movement carried him and Shawn across the drop between the two sections of the building. They landed in a crumpled heap on the floor of the other section. Chelsea's screams echoed in the air around them.

A flash of heat raced through Sydney's body bringing her to her knees. Nausea flared then a coldness filled her. Deathly cold. "Corrin!"

"No!" Orlaith screamed, anger and pain in equal amounts. The sound echoed around them.

Corrin struggled to his feet, a hand pressed against his left side. "We live."

"Corrin." Sydney's voice faltered as she saw the blood staining the hand he had pressed against his side. Still she felt no pain, no tightening of the skin. What had happened? Were they about to die?

Shawn swore as he rose unsteadily to his own feet. He looked around. "Where's Orlaith?"

Chelsea climbed down the side of the scaffolding. "She vanished. The man she was using fainted. We have to go. What if he wakes up and keeps doing what she wanted him to do?"

Chapter Twenty-Five

Sydney ran towards her friend and threw her arms around her. "Are you okay?" Surely one of them had to be fine. She didn't have a clue what state her and Corrin were in, but Chelsea had to be okay. She wouldn't accept anything else.

Chelsea nodded. "We have to get out of here."

Sydney's phone started to ring. She kept one arm around Chelsea as she pulled it from her pocket, swearing when she saw it was her mum calling. She pressed end and returned the phone to her pocket.

"She's going to freak," Chelsea warned.

"I'll call her as soon as we're out of here." Sydney looked across to Corrin and Shawn. "Corrin? How bad is it?" She eyed the blood staining his hand. Was this it? Were they both about to die? Then why was there no pain?

"I will be fine." Corrin looked behind him. "We have to return to Shawn's car."

"Wait a minute." Chelsea looked from Corrin to Sydney. "You're apart."

"The bond is broken," Corrin said.

"How?" Chelsea asked before Sydney had a chance to.

"I saved Shawn."

Relief hit Sydney. They weren't about to die. The coldness she felt wasn't death coming for her. But surely that wouldn't have been enough to end the spell.

Shawn took a step towards the edge, his gaze on Sydney. "Saving me broke the bond? Sydney? What does that mean? Have you made up your mind?"

Sydney shook her head. She could barely believe the fact she no longer had a Siamese twin let alone figure anything else out. "Let's get out of here." She tugged on Chelsea's hand as she started to turn away. "We'll meet you at the car."

"Sydney, what does it mean?" Shawn called after her.

Sydney ignored him as she returned the way they had come, pulling Chelsea with her. How could she answer a question she was still asking herself?

"What does it mean?" Chelsea asked.

Sydney shook her head with a shrug. "That my head is so screwed up that I haven't got a clue what's going on inside it."

"But the bond is broken, right?"

If Corrin said it was, she guessed it must be. Sydney nodded. All she felt was cold.

"It wouldn't break for just anyone, would it?"

Sydney shook her head.

Chelsea stopped moving, turning Sydney to face her. "Do you love him?"

"Chelsea! We have to get out of here. We don't know how long it will be before Orlaith returns. I don't even know why she disappeared. It's as good as dark and she isn't here." Sydney's phone started to ring again but she ignored it. "We have to go."

"Fine. But the moment we're safe you have to talk to me. I really thought you had a thing for Corrin." Chelsea grinned. "You do realise you can't have both of them."

Sydney rolled her eyes. "Come on." Maybe by the time they got home she might have figured out all the answers.

They reached the car to find Shawn already changing the tyre, muttering about the damage the trolley had caused. The homeless woman was no longer in sight, but her trolley still lay on its side on the road behind them.

Sydney went straight to Corrin who sat on the footpath, his hand pressed against his side. She knelt in front of him. "What happened?" Her gaze dropped to his bloodstained hand.

"I crashed into a metal stake that was sticking out of the floor."

"Is it bad? It looks like it's still bleeding." Sydney reached out to move his hand.

Corrin pushed her hand away before she could touch him. "I have had worse."

Chelsea joined them. "You need to see a doctor."

"Tyre's changed. Let's get out of here." Shawn held a hand out to Corrin. "And try not to bleed all over my car."

Corrin let Shawn pull him to his feet. "I do not think a bit of blood can make it look worse than the trolley did." He turned to enter the car.

"Corrin?"

Corrin turned to Shawn with a questioning look.

"Thanks."

Corrin nodded before he hopped in the car. Shawn walked around to the driver's seat.

Sydney turned to Chelsea with a grin. "It's sickening how they're gushing all over each other."

Chelsea laughed as she got in the front of the car.

Sydney dialled her mum's number the moment she buckled up and had to hold the phone away from her ear at the angry tirade. "Mum! If you shut up I can tell you what happened."

"Don't talk to me like that, Sydney."

"Yeah well it wasn't my fault we're late. Orlaith decided to take over a homeless woman and throw a trolley at the car. I couldn't answer the phone. We were trying not to get ourselves killed." Sydney waited for her mum to say something, but was greeted by silence. "Mum? You still there?"

"Where are you? Do we need to pick you up?"

"No. We're on our way home."

"Are you okay, Sydney? And the rest of you?"

"Yeah. Kinda. Corrin is bleeding, but he says it's not bad." Sydney's gaze was drawn to his wound.

"Sydney, if he should die-"

"We broke the bond."

"You're safe if he dies?"

"Apparently." But Sydney didn't feel in the least bit reassured. "Look Mum, I'll tell you everything when we get home. We'll be there as soon as possible."

"Be careful."

"Yeah." Sydney disconnected and returned the

phone to her pocket. "We need to take Corrin to the hospital."

"What is a hospital?" Corrin asked.

"A place of doctors or healers," Shawn said.

"When Sydney is safe."

"You don't have to worry about me anymore. We're no longer bound," Sydney said.

Corrin reached out with his clean hand and brushed it across her cheek. "Do you think me without honour?"

Sydney pushed his hand away. "Screw your honour. You need to see a doctor. Do you want to die?"

Corrin shook his head. "I need to get rid of Orlaith."

"And then what? You can die? Don't be an idiot. We have to go to the hospital." Sydney glared at him.

Corrin smiled. "So fierce. And stubborn. You would have done well in my world." He pressed his finger against her lips when she started to speak again. "Once you are safe then I will see your hospital."

Sydney brushed his hand away again. "Stop doing that. I'm not going to be quiet, but I will bite if you keep doing that."

Corrin's smile turned into a grin and his voice lowered. "Is that a promise?"

With a snort of disgust Sydney looked out the window, unable to focus on the passing surroundings. "Die then. See if I care."

"I'll take him to the hospital once I drop you and Chelsea at your place," Shawn said.

"But what if Orlaith-" Chelsea started to say.

Shawn interrupted her. "You'll be safe in the salt ring."

"It wasn't me I was worried about," Chelsea muttered.

"Forget it, Chelz. Guys are idiots no matter what century they're from."

When they reached Sydney's home, she started to get out of the car, but Corrin pulled her back. "What?"

"Stay inside."

"I'm not an idiot." Sydney gave him a scathing glare. "Unlike some people."

Corrin's reply was a grin.

Sydney started to pull away then turned back. "You make sure you get back here safely." She sent a look towards Shawn. "Both of you." She hopped out of the car and dropped her arm around Chelsea's shoulder as they headed for the front door.

Victoria and Malcolm burst outside, running towards them before they reached the door. Victoria wrapped her arms around the two of them, Malcolm drawing them inside where he insisted on hearing what had happened.

Victoria reached across the island bench, where they all sat in the kitchen, and took Sydney's hand. "You're certain the bond is completely broken?"

Sydney nodded.

"And you won't die if Corrin does?"

Sydney glared at her mum. "Stop talking about him dying."

"What I want to know is what happened to Orlaith," Malcolm said.

Sydney shrugged. "I don't know. I think she disappeared when our bond broke. But I don't know why, or for how long."

"I don't think she's gone for good," Chelsea said.

"Neither do I," Sydney agreed.

"We have to figure out what to do about her," Malcolm said. "And I don't think waiting for Theodore to come up with a solution is the answer."

When Sydney yawned, Victoria squeezed her hand. "Not tonight. I think it's time for showers and bed. For everyone. It's been a long day."

"But what about Corrin and Shawn?" Sydney asked.

"They know their way back here. But tomorrow

they can find another safe place to stay at night," Victoria said.

Chapter Twenty-Six

Sydney pulled away from her mum, rising to her feet. "No. Until Orlaith is dealt with we all stick together. I'd worry all night about what's happening. We can't afford to split up."

Victoria rose also. "Sydney be reasonable-"

"You be reasonable." She glared at her mum.

"Sydney's right. We don't want to split our forces."

Sydney and Victoria both turned towards Malcolm saying 'what' at the same time.

"This is war. You don't split your forces unless there's a strategic benefit. I can't see one." Malcolm held up his hand when Victoria started to speak. "But the boys can stay in the spare room and the girls in Sydney's room."

It was Sydney's turn to protest. The spare room, her old bedroom, was near the workshop. "Are you sure you don't want to make them sleep in the workshop? I mean that's further away than the spare room."

"No, the spare room will be far enough." Malcolm pushed away from the bench. "Now everyone off to bed. Your mum and I have to work in the morning."

Sydney retreated to her room with Chelsea, muttering under her breath about how unfair it all was. Once they had both showered, they sat on Sydney's bed so Chelsea could grill her.

Sydney had no answers and was relieved that before she had to answer a single question there was a knock at her sliding door. She pulled back the curtain. Corrin and Shawn stood there. Relief swamped her and she pulled open the door, throwing her arms first around Corrin then Shawn.

"You're both okay?" She stepped back to eye each of them. At their nods, she focused on Corrin. "What did the doctor say?"

Corrin closed and locked the sliding door, gesturing towards Shawn. "He tricked me into a blood test. I do not like your needles."

Shawn laughed. "Didn't you want to make sure you didn't bring any other diseases with you, other than Orlaith?"

Sydney closed her eyes momentarily. "Why are we having this discussion again?"

"At least you did not get lectured by the doctor and given pamphlets to read and condoms to use." Corrin held out the items he mentioned.

Sydney took a step backwards. "Don't give them to me."

Chelsea started to laugh.

"Then you take them." Corrin thrust them towards Chelsea who instantly stopped laughing.

She plucked the pamphlets from him. "Maybe you better keep the condoms. You never know when you might need them." She sent a quick look towards Sydney.

"Can I talk to you, Sydney?" Shawn asked. His gaze travelled around the room. "Alone?"

Sydney couldn't help glancing in Corrin's direction. His expression was unreadable. Sydney shook her head. "Not tonight. I'm tired."

"It'll only take a few minutes," Shawn said.

Sydney shook her head again. "Tomorrow." She moved towards her bedroom door. "My parents said you pair have to sleep in the spare room."

"I much preferred sharing your bed."

Sydney met Corrin's gaze then quickly looked away as she felt her cheeks heat. "There's only a single bed in there, but you can take one of the mattresses we used last night. We need to get one of them for Chelsea to sleep on too."

During the process of setting up for the night Sydney found herself alone in the hallway, near her room, with Shawn. "I can't do this right now."

"I nearly died earlier."

Sydney's gaze fell to the carpet near Shawn's feet. "I'm sorry."

Shawn stepped forward, his hands resting on her hips. "Look at me, Sydney."

She reluctantly met his gaze. She opened her mouth to ask him to wait until tomorrow when his lips met hers. She reached up to press her hand against his chest so she could push him away. The kiss was ended before she had a chance to.

Shawn stared at her a moment. "I guess I have my answer." He turned to move away.

"Shawn." She felt guilty for the pain she heard in his voice, but she couldn't give him the answer he wanted.

He stopped. His back still to her. "What?"

"I'm sorry."

He turned to face her. "Why did saving me break the bond?"

"I was so terrified when I saw you hanging there. I couldn't stand to think of you dying."

"Why?"

Sydney hesitated.

"Why?"

She couldn't bring herself to say the words. "It would devastate me if Chelsea died too."

"Sydney, just answer the question."

She took a step towards him, wishing she didn't have to speak. "It would hurt me to lose any friend."

Shawn grinned mirthlessly. "It's over, but let's remain friends?"

Sydney blinked several times, her throat tightening. "I'm sorry. But it isn't a line. You have to know that."

"Do I?"

She reached towards him. "Shawn-"

He took a step back. "Maybe we should leave this talk till tomorrow."

"If you meant nothing to me the bond wouldn't have broken."

"But what exactly do I mean to you?"

Again her gaze dropped to the carpet.

"You've chosen Corrin, haven't you?"

Her gaze quickly rose to meet his. "I haven't got a clue."

"Yeah, right."

Sydney shook her head. "I don't. I keep thinking-"

She broke off. This wasn't something she could say to an ex-boyfriend.

"Just say it. Aren't I meant to be a friend?"

Sydney ignored the mocking tone, forcing the words out. "I keep thinking it was all to do with the bond."

Shawn held her gaze a moment longer before he nodded with a wry smile. "I guess I asked for that." Again he turned away.

"Shawn?"

"What?"

"I'm glad you didn't die."

"Me too." He didn't look back as he headed down the hallway towards the spare room.

Sydney watched him walk away until he turned and stepped out of her sight. She leaned against the wall. Sorrow, confusion and fear swirled in her. Her eyes closed and she heard the bedroom door open and Chelsea's soft steps on the carpet.

"Are you okay?"

Sydney shrugged as she pushed away from the wall. "I need to sleep." She walked towards her bedroom door. "Wake me when this is all over."

Chelsea fell into step beside her. "What did Shawn want?"

"Why do I feel so bad that I broke it off with him?

I mean if I really wanted it to be over shouldn't I have been relieved? Not hurt?" Sydney closed her bedroom door behind them.

"Maybe it's because you didn't want to hurt him."

"I don't know." She dropped onto her bed. "Why is life so complicated?"

"Well, I hate to complicate things further–"

Sydney sat up and looked towards Chelsea who stood staring down at her. "What?"

"Mum rang me."

Sydney fell back against her bed. "Please. No more bad news."

"Okay."

Sydney sat up to see Chelsea settle herself on the mattress. She sighed. "What did she say?"

"I can't take up residence here."

"And?"

"She expects me home tomorrow night."

With a groan Sydney fell back against her pillow. "This isn't happening."

"What are we going to do?"

Hearing the fear in Chelsea's voice, Sydney slipped out of her bed and sat on the mattress, wrapping her arms around Chelsea, pressing her cheek against her friend's cheek. "Orlaith can't have you. We'll deal with it." She just wasn't sure how.

Chapter Twenty-Seven

Sydney was up before everyone, including her parents. Her broken sleep had her resting her head against the coolness of the benchtop, an untouched cup of hot chocolate beside her. Soft footsteps caused her heart to speed up and she turned to face the interruption. Seeing it was Corrin didn't help her heart drop back to its normal pace.

"Is all well?"

"Yeah, right. Just perfect. Orlaith would love to spend an eternity torturing me along with everyone I care about and Chelsea's parents expect her home tonight."

Corrin stopped behind her. "We will keep her safe."

Sydney turned back to her cup, fiddling with the warm handle. "How?"

"We have an entire day to prepare. We will

surround the house with a circle of salt like we did here."

She spun to face him. "I want everyone where I can see them. I want to know everyone is safe."

"Everything will be fine. Now finish your drink and stop worrying."

Sydney glared at him. "You drink it. And don't patronise me." She pushed past him.

"What is it?"

Sydney turned to see Corrin taking a mouthful of her drink. "Hot chocolate."

"It's good. How is it made?"

She stared at him. "We're all in danger and you're worried about how some stupid drink is made?"

Corrin put the cup on the bench and turned back to her with a smile. "All the more reason to enjoy every moment." He took a step towards her.

Sydney held up a hand when she recognised the look in his eyes. "Oh no you don't."

His smile didn't fade as he reached out to her. "Say that like you mean it."

"I really..." her words died away as his head lowered and her hand went from pushing against his chest to tangling in his hair, drawing him close. Their lips met and Sydney pressed herself even closer.

"Great, now my morning is perfect."

Sydney broke away from Corrin to face Shawn who stood at the hallway entrance. "Sorry."

"Oh don't mind me. Go back to it." He waved his hand towards them. "I just need coffee."

Sydney teetered between guilt and anger. She finally settled on anger as she watched Shawn fill the kettle. She swore at Shawn and turned away to see her parents step into the kitchen.

Victoria frowned. "Sydney."

Malcolm chuckled. "Trouble in paradise?"

"Paradise can be nuked for all I care." Sydney strode towards her bedroom and nearly ran into Chelsea as she opened the door. "Boys suck and should all be drowned at birth."

Chelsea rubbed at her eyes. "I'll help you after breakfast." She started to move away then stopped. "And coffee."

"Good. We can toss a coin to see which one goes first." Sydney grabbed a pair of jeans and a crop top before she headed for the bathroom, muttering threats under her breath.

* * *

Sydney stared at the dirt Shawn pushed into place

over the salt, sealing the area around Chelsea's house. She turned to her best friend. "You will be safe."

Chelsea nodded, her gaze drawn back to the disturbed ground. They had carefully replaced the grass in the hope her parents didn't notice, but the ground still looked disturbed.

"I'll have my laptop on all night. As soon as I get home I'm making a video call to you. And I'm not turning it off. If you even sneeze I'll know," Sydney warned.

Chelsea grinned. "You're starting to sound like a stalker."

Sydney slowly returned the grin. "That's okay. I need to know you're safe."

"I don't mind." Chelsea reached out and drew Sydney into a hug. "I wish there was some way to explain this to my parents."

Sydney's arms tightened around Chelsea. "Me too. But you will be safe. She can't cross the salt."

Chelsea checked the time on her phone. "You better go. My parents would freak if they got back to find a couple of strange guys hanging around here."

"Chelsea…" Sydney couldn't think what to say. She didn't want to leave.

"Go. None of us should be wandering around the

streets when it gets dark. I'll be okay. I'm going straight inside to turn my computer on," Chelsea said.

Sydney stared at her friend, noticing that the roots of her bleached hair were starting to show. "If anything–"

"Go. I'll be fine." Chelsea reached out and turned Sydney in the direction of home. "Go on."

Sydney spun to throw her arms around Chelsea. "Stay inside."

"You too."

Sydney reluctantly headed for home, glancing back at Chelsea who stood at her front door alone. Corrin and Shawn walked quietly beside her. She looked at the sky. Night was still a while away. They had to find a way to deal with Orlaith. She didn't know if she could cope with many more nights like this.

"What's wrong?" Shawn asked.

"Orlaith. What do we do when she's human? How will we protect ourselves then? Will the salt still work?"

Corrin shook his head. "Once she is human, my sword can end her life."

"She has a bow. How will you get close enough to use your sword against her?" Sydney asked.

"I have a shield."

"And it's four against one," Shawn said.

"We don't know anything about fighting," Sydney pointed out.

Shawn grinned. "And neither does Orlaith. Not in our time anyway. I'd bet on a gun against a bow any day of the week."

Sydney stopped to stare at him. "Where are we going to get a gun from? And I don't even know how to use one."

"I do. My dad and I used to regularly go to the shooting range when I was younger. He had plans to take me deer hunting one day. But 'one days' have a tendency never to arrive." There was a touch of bitterness in Shawn's voice.

"Are we planning to stand around here until it grows dark?" Corrin momentarily looked at the sky.

Sydney started walking again. "I want Orlaith dealt with before she's able to wander around by day. School starts next week. What if she walks into my classroom and kills me? Or some of my classmates."

"I doubt your parents would let you go to school if that was the case," Shawn said.

"I'm not going to spend the rest of my life locked up somewhere so Orlaith can't get me." Sydney led the way to the sliding door she'd left unlocked. "Besides, I'd fail school if I didn't go." She turned on her laptop and leaned against the edge of her desk as she waited for the programs to load. "Not that I know what I'm going to do when I've finished school."

"Join the club," Shawn muttered.

Corrin strode across the room to the bedroom door.

Sydney watched him open the door. "Where are you going?"

"Food."

Shawn followed Corrin. "I'll join you."

Sydney sat at her desk and logged into her messenger. Relief rushed through her when Chelsea immediately answered her video call. "You're okay?"

Chelsea nodded. "It's so quiet here. I want to run and check every little noise. I'm going to be a nervous wreck by morning."

"She can't cross the salt line."

"I know, but what if she's inside it?"

"Then you run over to my place."

"And leave my parents here with her?"

Sydney dropped her head into her hands, her elbows resting on the desk. "This is all too complicated."

"I'm sorry. I shouldn't have said anything."

Sydney raised her head. "Of course you should have. We all should have thought of it. But at least if your parents see Orlaith they'll believe you when you tell them about her."

"I guess." Chelsea didn't look convinced. "Anyway, enough with the boring stuff. What's happening with you and Corrin?"

"I wouldn't have a clue."

"Why not?"

Sydney fell silent, not sure how to answer. She shrugged. "I don't know."

"But you do like him?"

"Yeah."

Chelsea looked over her shoulder. "I think that's my parents." She rose from her desk and returned a minute later. "Yep. It's my parents. I better go and let them know I'm following orders. I'll be back in a little while."

"Okay. I'll go check what the boys are up to. They're raiding the kitchen, but they seem to be taking a really long time."

Chelsea grinned. "Maybe they're swapping notes."

"Great," Sydney muttered as she pushed away from her desk. Chelsea's laughter followed her out of the room as she headed to the kitchen. It was empty. A shout of victory drew Sydney to the rumpus room where she found Corrin and Shawn playing a game on the Xbox.

"I win. Again," Shawn crowed.

"If the sword fighting was more realistic you would be dead by now," Corrin said.

"Face it, you're hopeless at console games."

Corrin grinned. "Why do we not get a couple of practice swords and I'll show you what real sword fighting is about."

Shawn laughed. "Not likely."

"You will not always win. This game is easy to learn."

Shawn shrugged. "Then we'll play something else. Maybe a car racing game."

"Would that help me learn to drive a real car?"

Sydney stepped forward. "No. If you drove on the road like you do in a racing game the police would pull you over."

"Can you teach me to drive?" Corrin asked her.

She shook her head. "I don't have an open license."

"I bet Steve would teach you. He has an open license." Shawn grinned. "He'd probably swap driving lessons for sword fighting lessons."

Sydney looked from Shawn to Corrin, not sure that she liked how well they seemed to be getting along. Chelsea's comment of swapping notes came to mind. "You two are getting really friendly."

Shawn shrugged. "I can't exactly hate the guy who saved my life, even if he is after my girl."

"I'm not your girl."

"You were."

Sydney shook her head. "Fine. Whatever. I'm going back to my room." She strode away, trying not to feel annoyed that Shawn and Corrin now appeared to be friends. She entered her room and leaned against the door when she closed it. She sighed. How petty was she? Shouldn't she be glad Corrin was making friends? She heard a sound from her laptop and moved over to her desk in time to see Chelsea sit back down.

"I'm back."

"Me too." Sydney sat at her desk.

"What were the boys doing?" Chelsea grinned. "Comparing notes?"

"Playing on the Xbox."

"Seriously?"

Sydney nodded.

Chelsea shook her head. "Here we are trying not to die and they're playing games. I don't understand boys."

"Tell me about it." Sydney glanced towards her bedroom door. "I think my parents are home. I'll be back shortly."

"Okay. But don't be too long. I'm so bored. I can't believe I'm not allowed to stay at your place tonight."

Chapter Twenty-Eight

Sydney left her room in time to see her parents enter the front door. She reluctantly agreed to cook dinner and was surprised when both Corrin and Shawn helped her. After dinner they spent some time in Sydney's room talking to Chelsea. The door was open, according to orders from her parents, and the boys headed back to the spare room around nine. Sydney was left to pace her room, glancing frequently at the darkened room shown on her laptop screen.

"Are you still okay, Chelz?"

"Go to sleep, Sydney."

"I can't."

"Then go hassle the boys."

Sydney stopped in front of her laptop. "What if something happens while I'm gone?"

"I think we were worried about nothing. She's not in my house. Now let me sleep."

Sydney listened as Chelsea's bed creaked. She stared at the laptop a moment longer before she resumed her pacing.

There was a sigh from Chelsea. "Can you at least turn your light off? Or maybe put your bedside lamp on. I mean you won't let me cover my screen to stop the glare so it's the least you can do."

Before Sydney could answer, there was a tap on her bedroom door. She opened it to find Corrin and Shawn standing in the hallway. Shawn held his phone. "What's up?" She looked from one to the other.

"Sydney? What's happening?" Chelsea asked from the laptop.

Sydney stepped back so the boys could enter her room. She closed the door behind them. "I don't know." She strode back to her laptop where Chelsea's face now filled the semi darkness.

"Hurry up and tell me what's happening. I'm trying to sleep here," Chelsea complained.

"Ted rang," Shawn said.

"Really?" Chelsea turned a lamp on. "What did he have to say?" She blinked in the low wattage light.

"He's sending me an email. He doesn't want to

speak his thoughts aloud since he doesn't know who might overhear. It seems like the safest method when you consider the illiteracy factor," Shawn said.

"But Corrin can't read either," Sydney said. "Or has Ted left him out of his… thoughts?"

"Of course he hasn't. He'll have to wait until tomorrow to find out the details. I have a program on my computer that reads documents. He can use headphones," Shawn said.

"Isn't this a little extreme?" Chelsea frowned. "Surely Or-"

"Watch what you're saying," Shawn interrupted.

Chelsea rolled her eyes. "What are you worried about? Super sonic hearing or something?"

"We'll have one shot. We're not going to risk blowing it," Shawn said.

"When's he sending the email?" Sydney asked.

"He's already sent it." Shawn gestured towards Sydney's laptop. "I came in to ask if I can log into my email account and read it. I've run out of internet downloads on my phone."

"You better send a copy to me," Chelsea said.

Sydney nodded as she stepped away from the laptop so Shawn could use it. "Hurry up. I want to read it too."

Shawn reduced the size of the video call page and

opened a web browser. He quickly logged into his email account and forwarded a copy of the email to Chelsea, after Sydney had typed in her address. Sydney leaned over his shoulder to read the email.

She frowned. "He seems to have left a lot out."

"I guess there's things he didn't want to put in writing," Shawn said.

"Does it look like it will work?" Corrin asked.

Sydney glanced over her shoulder at him. "I think so." She frowned. "Maybe. I think some of it relies heavily on chance."

"No it doesn't. It relies on certain personality traits," Shawn said.

"Do you think it will work, Shawn?" Corrin asked.

Shawn hesitated then nodded. "Yeah. Some of it will involve luck, but yeah, I think it'll work."

"Me too," Chelsea said. "And I bet right about now you're wishing you could read, Corrin."

"I hope that putting these thoughts into words does not ruin our chances," Corrin said.

"Words aren't magic," Sydney said.

Corrin met her gaze. "Are you certain?"

Sydney started to say yes, then hesitated. Before Corrin she would have said magic wasn't real. What did she know? Instead she shrugged. "I've got to send a text to my parents so they don't ruin anything."

Corrin and Shawn returned to the spare room not long after Sydney had sent her text. The unspoken topic of Theodore's plan filled the room and no one had been able to focus on anything else.

Sydney finally drifted off to sleep, much to Chelsea's relief, waking several times throughout the night as she waited for morning. Over breakfast, her parents agreed to her request to be able to spend the day at the Boondall Wetlands. Then after a great deal of arguing, they also allowed her to go to a fictional party afterwards.

Chelsea was dropped off at Sydney's house by her parents, on their way to work, and she burst inside with a grin. "I can go, but I've got to be back home by one a.m."

Shawn put his breakfast plate in the sink. "That should give us plenty of time to," he paused and grinned. "Party."

"Forget about partying. I wish to use your computer," Corrin said.

Shawn nodded. "Shortly." He turned to Sydney and Chelsea. "You two coming?"

After a brief hesitation, Sydney shook her head. "You can pick us up on the way to the Wetlands."

As soon as the boys left, Chelsea turned to Sydney and grabbed her hands. "I'm so nervous."

"I know. Me too."

"I want to talk and discuss it and it's killing me that I can't say a word."

Sydney grinned. "Not long now."

"We have to do something to keep me from thinking. What can we do?"

"I wouldn't have a clue. I'm all out of ideas right now."

"Wow. I better mark this day down in my diary. The Master Of Plans has drawn a blank." Chelsea grinned.

Sydney made a face at her. "You could help me clean up the kitchen."

"Great." Chelsea's voice was heavily laced with sarcasm. "Just what I wanted to do." Even after her protests, Chelsea helped Sydney tidy up and then they got their gear ready for the day.

Sydney stared at her backpack. "Do you think I've got everything?"

"I don't know. I had the same problem when I was getting my stuff together this morning. At least you didn't have to worry about your parents saying no."

"Yeah, but you didn't have to convince your parents not to join you. You can't imagine the amount of texting I had to do this morning. It's hard when there are things you can't speak aloud. Especially when you're having an argument."

Chelsea laughed. "Okay, you win."

Sydney started to speak when she heard a car pull up outside. Her stomach lurched. "This is it." She reached out to take Chelsea's hands.

"Don't be nervous. A lovely day wandering the Boondall Wetlands is just what we need." Chelsea grinned. "It's the perfect place for a picnic. And there's lots of lovely walks for a couple to enjoy. You and Shawn should have a nice romantic day."

"Uh-huh. If you think so." Sydney's stomach didn't agree with Chelsea's light comments. She closed her eyes momentarily, her fingers tightening on Chelsea's. "Do you think we're doing the right thing?"

Chelsea nodded. "Now let's get out to the car before the boys are in here complaining about how long we're taking."

Chapter Twenty-Nine

Sydney reluctantly slid out of the backseat of Shawn's car. An entire day of exploring and learning their battleground didn't seem like a fun way to spend her time. Surely they didn't need that much time to finalise their plans. When she saw how vast the wetlands were, with their narrow paths, scrubby areas and salty patches, Sydney guessed they did need plenty of time to pick the perfect spot.

While they'd been at his house, Shawn had shown Corrin a couple of words to make communication easier. There was 'here', 'yes' and 'no'. Sydney almost yelled in victory when Corrin finally wrote the word yes. She looked around, her gaze drawn to the salt pan. It was several metres across, clumps of coarse grass around the edge, only a handful of trees in the area. The salt pan didn't seem like it would be a large enough battleground. And how were they going to get her onto it. There were too many things left to luck. Sydney wasn't sure her luck was all that good. Not lately anyway.

They stopped for a late lunch not far from their battleground and Shawn rang Theodore and read off the coordinates from his GPS. The conversation was extremely short and silence filled the area when Shawn disconnected.

They lazed about on the picnic blanket, half heartedly pointing out the different wildlife in the area. Sydney froze when Corrin, who was stretched out across the blanket from her, nudged her with his foot. She met his gaze. As soon as he had her attention, he gave a slight nod.

She wanted to protest. I'm not ready. The words rang in her head but she couldn't bring herself to say them. Instead she rose to her feet, surprised at how steady she was, and reached out a hand to Shawn. "Take a walk with me? I'm bored with lazing about."

Shawn allowed himself to be drawn to his feet, he glanced towards the sun that was nearing the horizon. "We should be going. It'll be dark soon."

Sydney shrugged. "So? She's gone. We haven't seen her since the bond was broken. Ask Chelsea. She saw Orlaith disappear."

Chelsea nodded, leaning back against her arms, her

elbows at the edge of the blanket. "Yep. Disappeared. We beat her." She grinned. "I didn't think it'd be so easy. I thought she'd come back, but-" she shrugged.

Shawn took a step away from the blanket, his fingers linked with Sydney's. "Maybe. But how can we be sure we've beaten her?"

"Forget her." Sydney tugged Shawn further from the blanket. "We're having the best day of the entire school holidays. Perfect weather. Great food. Relaxing day. I don't even want to think about her. You'll ruin my day. We won. Who cares about Orlaith? Not me."

"You better care."

Sydney spun to face Orlaith who leaned against a stunted tree. "Orlaith?" She tried to appear surprised. The satisfied expression on Orlaith's face made her think she might have achieved her goal.

Orlaith pushed away from the tree. "Did you miss me?" She moved forward till she stood in front of Sydney and Shawn. "You did not really think you had won that easily, did you? How pathetic." She spun around, her back to Shawn and Sydney. "All of you. Pathetic."

Sydney took the amulet Shawn handed her while Orlaith's back was turned and slid it into her pocket. "You're the one who's pathetic. You're only mist."

Sydney reached out and ran her hand through Orlaith forcing her to break up and reform a metre away from her. Sydney laughed. "We're going to have our walk, get in the car and go to a place where you can't reach us and there's nothing you can do about it. There aren't any people around here whose bodies you can take over." She took Shawn's hand, pulling him after her. "Come on." His hand felt hot and damp in hers. She bit back words of reassurance.

"Sydney, I don't–" Shawn began.

"Come on, Shawn." Sydney continued to draw him towards the correct spot as she turned to face him. She frowned, letting go of his hand to tug at the neck of his shirt. "Where's your amulet?"

Shawn's hand went to his throat and he looked around, turning rapidly. "It has to be here somewhere. I had it before lunch."

Corrin and Chelsea both rose to their feet. Sydney stepped away from Shawn while she looked around.

Orlaith laughed, breaking apart to appear in front of Shawn. "Nothing I can do about it? I think you are mistaken."

Shawn took a step away from Orlaith, his gaze focused on her. "Someone find my amulet. Hurry."

Orlaith reached up and ran a finger down Shawn's cheek. "Too slow. Much too slow."

Sydney wrapped her arms around herself as she watched Orlaith step into Shawn. His body shuddered and his eyes closed. Corrin threw himself at Shawn, tackling him onto the salt pan behind them both, landing hard on the ground. He threw the salt, he had hidden in his hands, over Shawn. Chelsea reached Sydney seconds later and they clung to each other as they watched.

Orlaith screamed. Anger. Pain. Wordless noise that filled the air and startled a flock of birds into the sky. She crouched on the ground beside Shawn who rolled away from her, salt drifting from his arms and shirt. Corrin leapt to his feet, dragging Shawn from the misshapen patch of ground. Sydney finally broke away from Chelsea to slip the amulet over Shawn's head and he wrapped his arms around her.

She started to pull away from him. "Shawn–"

"No. Give me a minute. Please."

Sydney silently held onto him, trying to ignore Orlaith who continued to scream and yell. "Are you okay? Did she hurt you?"

"No. Not exactly." Shawn started to draw away.

Sydney grabbed his arm, keeping him from moving away from her. "What does that mean?"

Shawn shook his head, tugging his arm from her grasp. "I've got to ring Ted." He walked several metres away, taking his phone from his pocket, his fingers reaching up to brush against his amulet.

Sydney turned to Corrin who rummaged through their items spread out on the picnic blanket. "What are you doing?"

He straightened with a grin, a handful of salt in one hand, a container full in the other. "Getting rid of that noise." He strode to Orlaith and flung the handful of salt at her. She screeched even louder from where she crouched on the ground, as if about to spring up at him. "Do you want more?" He tipped out another handful and prepared to fling it at her. "Quiet or I will continue to throw salt at you."

Orlaith fell silent, still crouched on the ground, glaring up at Corrin. "Pray to the gods I do not manage to leave this salted ground. You will not live to draw another breath."

"What about making me suffer?" Corrin tipped the salt from his hand into the container when Orlaith, barely moving, turned her back to him. She remained huddled close to the ground.

Chelsea retreated to the picnic blanket where Sydney and Corrin joined her. She gestured towards Orlaith. "Are you sure that'll keep her?"

Corrin nodded. "She can barely move. You saw her. She cannot leave the salt pan."

"But what about when it's dark?" Chelsea's gaze was again drawn to Orlaith.

"Then she will be in more pain. She is barely human at the moment. After dark she will have no choice but to be fully human, unable to return to her spirit form." He looked towards the horizon. "Not much longer now."

Sydney started to pack up their gear. "I can't wait for all this to be over." She stopped as Shawn walked towards them.

"Ted said he'll ring when it's time to meet him." Shawn tucked his phone away. "Soon. It's getting darker." His gaze was first drawn to the last glimpse of sun on the horizon and then to Orlaith. "This better work." His fingers again brushed his amulet.

"It will," Corrin said.

Shawn ran his hands through his hair. "I can't do that again." He began to move away.

"She would not fall for the same trick," Corrin said.

Shawn's steps slowed as Corrin spoke then sped up to move away from them.

Chelsea reached out to Sydney, a hand on her forearm. "Should we go after him?"

Sydney stared at his retreating figure. "I don't know."

"Corrin and I can finish packing up." Chelsea

looked down at the picnic blanket then back at Sydney. "Are you certain Shawn didn't get hurt?"

Sydney shrugged. "I don't know." She watched Orlaith, who still had her back to them. "I'll go and find out." She walked over to Shawn who sat on the ground, leaning against a tree. She stood looking down at him, unsure how to start.

Shawn finally looked up at her. "What?"

She took that as an invitation to sit beside him. "Are you sure you're okay?" She began to think he wouldn't answer and tried to think of something else to say.

"I almost fought him."

"Don't you mean her?"

Shawn shook his head then looked at her, his face in shadow. "Corrin. I barely managed to stop myself from fighting him. From dodging or running. Anything to stop him."

"Stop him?" Sydney frowned.

"Invincible. That's how she made me feel. Like I could do anything. Be anything. Powerful. And it was all I could do to stand there and let him take that feeling away." Shawn drew his legs up and rested his arms on them, his chin on top of his arms. "It's the hardest thing I've ever had to do."

Chapter Thirty

Sydney reached out to rest her hand on his shoulder. "But you didn't. You stood there and let Corrin drive her from you."

"Why him?" Shawn lifted his head to look at her. "Why?"

"I don't know." Her words were soft, reluctant. "I didn't expect it. I mean, I was determined to stay with you, but..." she couldn't think of a way to explain.

"I screwed it up."

"Maybe we both did."

Shawn sighed heavily and rested his chin on his arm again. "I just want this over."

Sydney couldn't help smiling. "Me too."

"I hope the rest of Ted's plan works. I don't know why he couldn't put it in the email."

Sydney jumped as Shawn's phone started to ring. "I guess we're about to find out."

"Yeah?" Shawn listened a moment. "Okay." He disconnected. "Time to go. He's not far from here. We're to look for the paper lantern." He rose to his feet and held out a hand.

Sydney took his hand and let herself be drawn upwards. "Paper lantern?"

Shawn shrugged, the movement barely noticeable in the twilight. "Come on. Let's get this over and done with."

"Shawn?"

He turned back to her and waited.

"You won't… I mean we'll… will…" Sydney looked at her feet, the shadows making the ground indistinct.

"Just say it, Sydney."

"Friends. I don't want to lose your friendship when this is all over."

"Let's just get through tonight." He turned away and strode towards Corrin and Chelsea.

Sydney watched him go and pressed a hand to her stomach. She took a shaky breath and let her hand fall to her side as she put one foot in front of the other. Her hands itched to take Corrin's salt container. Orlaith had wrecked everything. Ted better have a really good plan. Chelsea stepped forward to grab her hands as she reached them and

Sydney's heart gave a lurch. What did Ted have in mind? They couldn't leave Orlaith in the wetlands forever.

Chelsea's grip tightened on Sydney. "I'm just about shaking."

Sydney could only nod.

"I hope he doesn't expect me to do too much. I'd probably stuff it up I'm so nervous."

"Come on." Shawn strode across the uneven ground, a torch now held in his hand.

"I think I'm going to be sick." Chelsea let go of one of Sydney's hands to splay her hand across her stomach. "Maybe I should have skipped lunch."

Sydney took the torch that Corrin held out to her and turned it on, the beam pointed at the ground. She tugged Chelsea forward, following Corrin who strode after Shawn.

"Sydney?"

She glanced at Chelsea.

"You okay?"

A nod.

"You sure?"

Another nod.

Chelsea came to a sudden stop. "Oh god! We're going to fail. Even you're scared witless."

Sydney forced herself to speak. "Get a grip. Now

hurry up. Shawn's getting too far ahead of us. We don't want to leave Orlaith alone any longer than we have to." She tugged Chelsea forward, following Corrin who had stopped when they had. Shawn was well ahead of the three of them. She hoped it wouldn't take too long to find Theodore. If she didn't learn what the plan was soon, she was going to scream with frustration. It had to work. Whatever he had organised just had to work. Her feet slowed when she saw Theodore ahead of her.

He held a paper lantern on a long stick, a sign in the other hand. Behind him followed four dark garbed people carrying a coffin. As they drew closer Sydney was able to read the glow-in-the-dark writing on the sign. 'Please show respect to our father's last request by not disturbing this procession.' Her mouth dropped open and she slowed to a complete stop. But it was Chelsea who spoke the words she was thinking.

"What on earth has he got planned?"

Sydney could only shake her head, finally able to close her mouth. The four people lowered the coffin as Shawn reached Theodore. She hurried forward, not wanting to miss a second of the explanation, Chelsea at her side. They reached him just behind

Corrin. Theodore shook hands with his companions after he had pushed his sign into the ground.

"Thanks for your help with my research."

"No problems. Let us know how it goes. Should be interesting to read. Especially when you do the city procession." The young man slipped off his black suit coat and handed it over to Shawn. "Here ya go. I should warn you that coffin might be empty but it certainly gets heavy after awhile."

Shawn took the suit coat with a nod and slipped it on, buttoning it up. The other three also handed over their suit coats, a small man gave his to Chelsea while the only female in the group gave hers to Sydney. She looked at each stranger, surprised to see they all were similar in clothing sizes as her friends. She hoped Theodore's attention to detail continued.

As soon as the four strangers left, Shawn demanded, "What's the plan?"

"Is she far from here?" Theodore glanced in the direction they had come from.

Shawn shook his head. "No. But we do need to know what's going on."

"I'll tell you while we walk. If you could all pick up the coffin." Theodore pulled his sign from the ground. The moment they started walking he began to speak. "I used the idea of salt that you talked about.

This coffin is lined so nothing can get in or out to dissolve the salt. She'll be completely packed in salt and buried."

"What's to stop someone from digging her up?" Sydney asked.

"Like a dog digging up a bone," Shawn muttered.

"She'll be set in concrete."

"How did you manage that?" Chelsea asked.

"It didn't take too much organising. The base and sides are poured and will be set by the time we arrive. I want her completely surrounded in concrete. There's a concrete slab for the lid. We should be able to lift it on between the five of us. Then we'll cover that with dirt, put the rio back in place and in the morning the building site won't know the difference. Their load of concrete will be poured and a multi story shopping centre built over it. But just in case she's ever dug up, I've put a letter inside that's been laminated."

Sydney stared at the back of Theodore's head. Maybe he'd been watching too many crime movies. "How did you find out about the concrete being poured? And how did you get the base and sides done?"

"I said it was for a time capsule. A lot of people

do them now. And I got different people to help out. People who wouldn't be too curious," Theodore said.

Chelsea rubbed at her arm. "This coffin does get heavy. How far do we have to carry it to get back to your car?"

"Hearse."

Sydney shuddered. "I hope you don't expect any of us to get in the hearse with you."

Theodore laughed as he planted his sign in the ground near Orlaith. "You'll face down an evil spirit, but you won't get in a hearse?"

"I didn't have a choice about dealing with her." She met Orlaith's glare from where she still crouched on the ground.

Theodore pulled out a filled hypodermic needle. "Well someone needs to deal with her again. As long as you're certain she's human now."

Corrin nodded. "It is dark. She's human. Still part spirit, but human enough."

"Who's going to hold her?" Theodore asked.

Corrin stepped into the circle and pinned Orlaith to the ground. She bucked and screeched the moment he did. Shawn hesitated but quickly joined him. As soon as she was completely pinned, Theodore injected her. He stepped back out of the salt pan.

"You can let her go." Theodore recapped the needle and returned it to his pocket. "Not long now."

"This is too easy," Chelsea said.

"It's about time something was." Sydney watched as Orlaith's eyes closed and she slumped against the ground. She didn't look so dangerous now she was in a crumpled heap. But Sydney knew that with Orlaith looks were deceiving. She would kill them if they failed to deal with her tonight. There'd be no more games.

Within minutes they had her and her weapons in the coffin and Theodore packed her sedated body in salt. He placed the laminated letter on top of her before he closed the coffin. They collected their gear and started back to the hearse. By the time they reached it, Chelsea was muttering about her aching arms. They had stopped several times to change sides. Luckily they had passed no one, and Theodore told them about the supposed paper he'd told his earlier helpers he planned to write. It was about how people reacted to the trappings of death in unusual places. He was starting to think it would actually make an interesting paper to research.

Once they reached the building site, they waited for Theodore to confirm that everything was fine before they took the coffin to the prepared hole.

Sydney stared down at the coffin snug in the concrete box.

"Hurry up." Theodore glanced around nervously. "We have to get this done before the security guard does his rounds." He checked the time. "We've got just under an hour."

Sydney pushed against the slab of concrete that lay in the dirt beside the hole. Even with the cylindrical lengths of timber under it they had trouble moving the lid into place. Sweat poured down the side of her face and she wanted to stop and wipe it away. But she couldn't. The lid was only half on.

Theodore swore as he straightened. "That's the guard's vehicle pulling up out the front. He's early."

Chapter Thirty-One

Sydney straightened too, glad Theodore hadn't let them use their torches. Luckily starlight, moonlight and streetlight prevented total darkness. "We have to do something."

"Did you get the spare tyre fixed?" At Shawn's nod, Chelsea held out her hand. "Give me the car keys."

"What for?" Shawn was still crouched by the stone slab.

"Quit arguing. Do you want to be caught?" Chelsea snatched the car keys and turned to Sydney. "Ask him to help change a tyre. I'll meet you there."

Sydney grinned. "Now who's making plans like a master?"

"I'm just terrified about being stuck in a detention centre." Chelsea looked back at the boys. "Make sure you hurry up. I don't know how long we'll be able to stall him." She ignored Shawn's grumbles as she cut across the building site in the darkest shadows.

With a deep breath, Sydney circled around, coming towards the security guard from the direction of the road. As she strode towards him, she practiced in her head what she'd say to him. Sliding her hands into her suit coat, she wished she'd removed it earlier. It wasn't exactly normal attire.

"Who's there?" The security guard swung the beam towards her.

Sydney shielded her eyes. "I'm sorry, I didn't mean to startle you. I need some help. We've got a flat tyre and I don't know how to change it. I tried to ring my dad, but his phone keeps going to his message bank."

"You shouldn't be here." He pointed the light towards the ground.

"I'm sorry, but we're stuck out here alone."

"We?" The guard looked around.

"My friend. I told her to wait at the car. We've been stuck on the side of the road for ages. I swear there's never a cop around when you need one and then we saw you. I mean security guards are just like private cops, aren't you?"

"I wouldn't have put it like that." His hand went to the back of his neck, the beam of light now pointed directly down. He rubbed his neck then looked around again.

"Please say you can help us. I don't know how long before my dad answers his phone. I'm beginning to think he's let the battery go flat again." Sydney took a few steps closer. "I swear if we're stuck around here all night I'm going to have a heart attack. Do you know how many unexplained noises there are in the dark?" She mentally winced as she heard one of them off to her right. "Millions. Absolutely millions."

"Well…"

"You will?" She tried to sound extremely enthusiastic with a good dash of relief. "Really?"

He shone his torch on his watch. "It shouldn't take too long and I guess I am running ahead of schedule tonight."

"Oh, thank you. You can't imagine how grateful I am." Sydney gestured in the correct direction. "We're parked over that way." The guard fell into step beside her. "You are an absolute lifesaver, did you know that?"

"I'd suggest getting your dad to show you how to change a tyre first thing tomorrow. It's something everyone should know how to do."

"Absolutely." Sydney nodded vigorously. "First thing. I'm never getting stuck like this again. This is one of the worst things that's ever happened to me." She gestured towards Shawn's car. "Here we are."

Chelsea moved away from the car to throw her arms around Sydney. "You were gone forever. What if some axe wielding murderer had been about?"

The guard snorted. "I think you girls have been watching too many horror movies."

"How did you know that's where we've been?" Chelsea stared at him.

Sydney bit back a grin as she followed Chelsea's lead. "I didn't tell him. And I swear I'm avoiding horror movies from now on."

The guard shone his light on the flat tyre. "So where's the spare?"

Sydney shrugged. "I don't know. I guess it's in the boot."

"I'll have a look." Chelsea walked to the boot and opened it with the keys she held. She peered inside. "I need some light."

The guard strode forward and shone his light into the boot. With Sydney and Chelsea's hindrance, he finally got the tyre changed and they thanked him profusely as he tried to disentangle himself from their enthusiastic handshakes. He finally managed to move away and the girls waved and called out thank you several more times.

As soon as the guard was out of earshot, Sydney turned to Chelsea. "I hope they've had enough time to get everything done."

Chelsea checked the time on her phone before she slid it into her pocket. "That must have been the slowest ever tyre change. You were absolutely inspired when you dropped the wheel nut."

Sydney grinned. "I know. He was far too efficient." A movement out of the corner of her eye had her spinning around, pressing a hand against her heart as she saw the three boys step out of the shadows. "You lot nearly frightened the life out of me. Is it done?"

Theodore nodded. "Yes. And I have a place organised where I can watch and make sure nothing goes wrong."

"I didn't think about that," Sydney said.

"I will watch with you," Corrin said.

"Me too," Sydney and Chelsea said together.

"You have to be home by one," Shawn reminded Chelsea.

"So? I can watch till then."

"We can sort it out later. Right now we have to get away from here before the guard leaves." Theodore nodded towards the building site.

Ten minutes later the five of them were seated on the balcony of an empty apartment, not far from the building site, with a pair of night vision binoculars. Corrin turned them over in his hands as he examined them.

"How did you know about this place?" Sydney leaned against the rough brick wall and tried unsuccessfully to get comfortable.

"It was in the 'to let' notices of the local newspaper." Theodore took the binoculars off Corrin and looked through them, pointing them at the place they had buried the coffin.

They fell silent, each of them regularly taking turns to check the building site. As midnight approached Sydney sent a text message and was surprised to receive a call from her parents. The conversation was short since she didn't want to explain anything on the phone. Then it was time for Shawn to drive Chelsea home. He returned once she was dropped off.

Sydney started to fall asleep, jerking awake when she began to lean sideways. Corrin moved over to sit beside her and she rested her head on his shoulder. When she noticed Shawn's gaze on her, she closed her eyes. She drifted off to sleep again, only to be woken by a whispered discussion. Her eyes blinked as she tried to focus in the early morning light.

"What's going on?" Sydney covered her mouth as she yawned.

"They're pouring the concrete." Shawn turned towards her with a grin and offered her a different set of binoculars.

She moved to the edge of the balcony and looked through them. She held her breath as she checked where Orlaith was buried. A large cement truck was backed up to the area and a chute poured wet concrete over the ground. "It's over? She can't get out?"

"She's in there for good," Theodore said.

"But-" Sydney hesitated. "I mean, I know she's an evil spirit…" her voice trailed off as she tried to think of how to word her question.

"If you're getting cold feet it's a bit too late to worry about it now," Shawn said. "I don't know about you but I'm not going to lose any sleep over her. She's dead. And she didn't manage to put an arrow through me."

"I know, but-"

Corrin interrupted Sydney. "She will fade to nothing eventually. She is trapped by the salt and it will make her lose the power she has gained."

"And then she'll be truly dead?" At Corrin's nod she looked through the binoculars again. "Forever. No coming back?" She turned to face him.

"No coming back."

"How long will this take?"

Corrin shrugged. "It will depend on how strong she is. A few years. A few decades." He shrugged. "Longer." His lips slowly curved into a smile. "But I do not plan to dig her up to find out."

Sydney shuddered and looked through the binoculars again. The workmen were starting to smooth out the slab. "I can't believe it. I think it's going to take a while for it to sink in."

"Don't hog the binoculars." Shawn reached out for them.

"How long should we watch?" Sydney continued to stand at the balcony rail, her hands wrapped around the cold metal.

"Until the concrete is hard," Theodore said.

Chapter Thirty-Two

They stood together, one on each side of her, arms occasionally brushing as they shared the binoculars. Theodore paced behind them, muttering and scribbling, sometimes asking for a turn with the binoculars. Chelsea rang mid morning and her parents rang at lunchtime while Shawn was off buying take away food. Theodore was the first to leave early in the afternoon, making Shawn promise to return the binoculars and not to leave until the end of the workday.

When the workers left the site at the end of the day, Sydney almost ran to the car. She replied to Chelsea's last text as she slid into the front seat of Shawn's car, also speaking the words she had sent out loud. "I never want to go through another day like that."

Shawn started the car. "I'll come by in the morning and check that everything is still fine with the slab."

"And there will be no reason for this concrete to be broken?" Corrin asked.

"Not unless we've got really bad luck." Shawn pulled up at a red traffic light.

Sydney grinned. "Considering he's meant to be dead I'd have to say Corrin has plenty of good luck."

"I'm beginning to think he's got really good luck." Shawn met Corrin's gaze momentarily in the rear view mirror. "Dillon moved in with his girlfriend so we've got a spare room. Apparently we're inconsiderate and think of no one but ourselves." Shawn grinned. "But the room's there if you want it. We can talk rent and stuff later. I'm sure the guys can hold off for a couple of weeks while we sort out identity and some sort of work for you."

Corrin nodded slowly. "If you would not mind I will take that offer. Mal explained that when there is no more danger I must leave his house."

"They can't expect you to sleep on the streets," Sydney exclaimed.

"I will not be on the street. I'll stay at Shawn's house."

Sydney twisted in her seat to look at Corrin. She didn't want him to move out. She reached between the front seats to rest her hand on his denim clad knee. "I don't-"

"Come on you pair. Can't you wait until I'm not around?" Shawn interrupted.

Sydney drew back her hand. "Fine." They pulled up in front of her house and she hopped out when the car had barely stopped moving.

"Sydney. Wait." Shawn turned off the engine and hurried after her. "I'm sorry. We're all tired. I didn't mean to snap."

She turned to face him with a soft sigh. "Yeah. I'm tired too." She glanced behind her when she heard the front door open. "And I've still got my parents to face. I bet they'll have a million questions."

"I will answer them." Corrin strode across the front yard and stopped in front of her parents.

Sydney faced Shawn. "Are you okay? Are we still-"

"Not right now. Give me a couple of days."

"I hate waiting. For anything." She tried to glare but she was too tired to make much of an effort.

Shawn grinned. "I know." His phone beeped and he checked the screen. His grin became a laugh. "Hey, Corrin." He walked partway across the yard. "You know how we were discussing your luck earlier? Well your results from the hospital came back. You're all clear."

"What results?" Victoria asked.

Sydney shoved at Shawn's upper arm with the base of her palm. "Really? Do you have to?"

He laughed as he held up a hand in surrender and stepped quickly away from her as she reached out to shove him again. "Yep."

"What results?" Victoria asked again.

"Nothing," Sydney muttered. She turned to Corrin. "Do you need your gear?"

"Where's he going?" Malcolm asked.

"To Shawn's house," Sydney said.

"I hope he's not planning to take all that valuable jewellery. He really should put it in the safe," Victoria said.

It was Sydney's turn to laugh. "Great Mum. Kick him out, but let his jewellery stay. Real nice."

"Sydney–" Victoria began sternly.

"I would be glad to have my jewellery put in the safe," Corrin said.

Victoria nodded. Her and Malcolm stepped out of the doorway. "You had better come in and get your things. You probably all need an early night."

"I'll wait at the car." Shawn strode towards his car and leaned against the passenger door, his feet resting on the concrete edge of the gutter.

Sydney led the way to her room, closing the door once Corrin was inside, ignoring her mum's order to leave it open. She stared up at Corrin. All the words that had spun inside her head on the drive home evaporated. She continued to stare.

Corrin smiled slightly and reached out to run his fingers across her cheek. "I will see you tomorrow." His lips met hers and lack of words became unimportant. As did time.

They were dragged apart by the banging on Sydney's bedroom door. "Hurry up. You don't need all night to collect a handful of items." There was a moment of silence before the sound of Victoria's footsteps sounded in the hallway.

Corrin's fingers were still tangled in Sydney's hair, a slight smile on his lips. "I should leave before your father comes in here."

Sydney slowly nodded, but her arms stayed wrapped around his waist.

His smile widened and he swiftly kissed her before he stepped away to take his gear from the wardrobe, including his weapons. "I will see you tomorrow."

Sydney nodded and watched as Corrin opened her bedroom door. He stepped into the hallway. "Corrin?"

He turned, his gaze on her as he waited for her to continue.

"That wasn't because you were… I don't know… grateful? That kiss."

Corrin crossed the space between them, his gear dropping to the carpet so he could cup her face in his hands. "I am grateful, but the kiss was because I wanted to." He kissed her again and this time it was Malcolm at the open bedroom door who broke them apart. Corrin stared down at her with a smile, before he gathered his gear and strode from the room.

"You know he's far too old for you," Malcolm said.

Sydney stared at her dad for a moment then shook her head. "No, I think it's because he's far too serious for you."

"Sydney-"

She shook her head again. "I'm tired, I've buried a living spirit and I don't have the energy for a fight. Not to mention I'm still getting used to the idea that someone is no longer trying to kill me with an arrow."

"We worry about you-"

Sydney held up her hand. "Please. No more tonight. I really need a hot shower and a long sleep." For a moment she thought her dad would continue to speak.

He nodded. "Goodnight, sweetheart." He stepped

into the room and wrapped his arms tightly around her. "I love you."

"Love you too, Dad." She momentarily rested her head against his shoulder before she drew away from him. She watched him leave, closing the door as he went. After staring at the closed door for a few moments, her gaze was first drawn to her bed, then to the doorway of her ensuite. The bed looked very tempting, but in the end she had a short shower followed by the long sleep she needed.

Chapter Thirty-Three

At the sound of the car horn, Sydney ran towards the front door. It was the last day of the school holidays and the four of them were going to spend it at the beach. Her parents were a lot more tolerant of Shawn now they knew she was no longer interested in dating him. She grinned as she opened the front door, her backpack slung over one shoulder. They would have been even happier if she listened to them regarding their concerns about Corrin. Since he was working part time making jewellery for their boss and learning how to read and write, it was hard for them to come up with serious objections. It also helped that they both liked him and his ability for making jewellery.

Corrin pushed open the car door for Sydney as she approached it and slid across the back seat to make room for her. He reached out to run the backs of his fingers across her cheek, smiling.

"Not in my car. I'm starting to sound like a scratched CD. Do I have to say this every time?" Shawn asked.

Sydney grinned. "I guess we'll find out." Her grin widened in response to the one Chelsea sent her.

"We'll see." Shawn pulled out onto the road.

He still hadn't told Sydney if they'd remain friends, but so far he hadn't left her life either. She turned to Corrin. "Miss me?"

Corrin nodded. His thumb brushed the shadows under her eyes. "Are you okay?"

She nodded. "Bad dreams. I guess I can't bury them as easily."

"Dreams can be portents," Corrin said. "A forewarning of what is to come."

"No they can't. Just like written words can't cause a plan to fail. Now stop worrying about it. A few bad dreams are to be expected. This is the last day of the school holidays. I plan to think about nothing other than sand, sea and sun."

"Nothing else?" Corrin's voice dropped. "Nothing?"

Sydney tried to keep the smile off her face. She

couldn't stop it. "Well, maybe one or two other things."

"Please! I'm sitting right here. Can't you pair wait?" Shawn demanded.

Chelsea giggled.

Shawn snorted. "I swear I'm just a taxi service, and an unpaid one at that."

Still smiling, Sydney leaned against Corrin, relaxing into his warmth. Her eyes closed as Chelsea turned up the radio when it started to play one of her favourite songs. The rest of the drive to the beach was mostly quiet.

They'd been in the ocean for a couple of hours before Sydney splashed through the waves, heading to the shore, to drop onto her towel she'd left spread on the beach. The other three were still in the water. Shawn soon joined her.

He reached into the esky and pulled out a can of soft drink. "You want one?"

Sydney shook her head. She wondered if she should ask him yet again. Her gaze followed his movements as he opened the can and took a mouthful.

"Are you going to stare at me the entire time I drink this?"

Sydney grinned. "Nope. Just until you answer my question."

Shawn started to smile. "Only one question?"

"For now."

His smile faded. "Yeah. We're still friends. Surprisingly."

"Why surprisingly?"

"Because I was angry with you for a while."

"And now you're not?"

"Not much." Shawn shrugged. "And I can't be angry with the guy who was injured saving my life." His gaze was drawn to Corrin and Chelsea, who were still in the water. "I tried, but it didn't work. Besides, he's actually pretty interesting to be around." He grinned wryly. "Sometimes I'm tempted to introduce him to mates as my ex-girlfriend's boyfriend just to see their reaction."

Sydney laughed. "Yeah, I can see you doing that."

"I've been going over some of my old school assignments with him trying to teach him stuff and it's made me think about going back to uni."

"And do what?"

"Continue my law degree." He grinned. "My parents agreed to foot the bill, but I agreed only if I could minor in history. It's not such a bad subject."

"I thought you hated law."

Shawn shrugged. "So did I. Things change I guess." He glanced down at his multicoloured nails. "Well, not everything."

Sydney grinned. "I hope not." She'd always admired his unique style.

"Corrin's interested in some of the history units. You never know. He might end up lecturing at uni one day, about the time of his beginnings."

She reached out and tapped the amulet Shawn still wore. "How are you doing? No nightmares?"

"None. Now." He ran his fingers over the amulet. "You should wear yours."

"Why?"

"It'll help with the dreams."

Sydney hesitated. She needed to ask a question, but she wasn't sure she wanted to hear the answer. She sighed. "Do you think she's still kind of free?" She held her breath, waiting for his answer.

Shawn shook his head. "No. I just think she can still reach us a bit. We were the ones closest to her. You set her free. I used my body to trap her in the salt pan."

"It makes sense. But what about my mum and the other people she possessed?"

"I don't know. Your mum wasn't possessed for

long and the others," he shrugged. "I don't think they were important to her. Give the amulet a try."

She slowly nodded. "Okay." Laughter drew her gaze back to the water. Sydney's gaze fell on Corrin as he walked up the beach towards her, Chelsea at his side. She returned Corrin's smile then turned to Shawn when he groaned. "We're not in your car now."

"Yeah, but this is a public place. There's little kids on this beach. You'll psychologically scar them for life," Shawn said.

Sydney rose to her feet, smile still in place. "Them or you?"

"Both?"

"Both what?" Chelsea asked as she reached them.

Sydney shook her head. "Never mind." She turned to Corrin with a grin. "Do you want to come for a walk?" She sent a look towards Shawn when he groaned again. He grinned unrepentantly. She turned back to Corrin. "Well?"

Corrin nodded and linked his fingers with Sydney's as they walked along the beach, avoiding the scattered groups of people. "You and Shawn seem easier with each other."

Sydney nodded. "Yeah. I think he's ready to forgive me." She frowned. "Or should that be us?"

Corrin let go of her hand to slide his arm around her waist and draw her in closer. "Us."

She glanced up at him. "We haven't really spoken about that."

"About what?"

"Us."

Corrin grinned as he stopped walking to stare down at her, his other arm encircling her waist too. "Who needs words?" His lips met hers and her arms slid around his neck.

She agreed. Who needed words?

Free Ebook

Subscribe to Avril's newsletter to receive a free ebook. This ebook is exclusive to those on her mailing list. To find out more about this offer visit: http://www.avrilsabine.com/free-ebook/

*

We value your privacy and will not sell, rent, exchange or loan your email address to third parties. Your information is confidential and you are under no obligation to remain on the mailing list and can unsubscribe at any time.

Acknowledgements

Many thanks to the usual crew.

To The Reader

If you enjoyed this book, why not consider leaving a review to help other readers discover it too? Reader engagement is one of the few ways that lets an author know readers want more books in a particular series or genre. So leave a review and tell friends, not only about this book but also about other ones you've enjoyed, so you can continue to enjoy books by your favourite authors for years to come.

Dreams are meant to be lived,

Avril.

About The Author

Avril is an Australian author who lives with her family on acreage in South East Queensland. She writes mostly young adult speculative fiction, but has been known to dabble in other genres. You can find more information about her at her website www.avrilsabine.com where you can also subscribe to her newsletter to be kept informed about new releases, current projects, blog posts and exclusive news.

Titles By Avril Sabine

Stories about strong characters and characters who discover their strengths.

SERIES

Assassins Of The Dead- Young Adult Fantasy/ Paranormal

Book 1: Dark Blade

Book 2: Dragon Touched

Book 3: Society Against Vampires

Book 4: King's Request

Dragon Blood- Young Adult Urban Fantasy (with elements of romance)

(5 book series)

Book 1: Pliethin

Book 2: Wyvern

Book 3: Surety

Book 4: Knight

Book 5: Mage

Dragon Mage- Young Adult Urban Fantasy (with elements of romance)

(Series two of Dragon Blood series)

Book 1: Promise

Dragon Blood Chronicles- Young Adult Urban Fantasy (with elements of romance)

(Companion stand alone series to Dragon Blood)

Book 1: Oath

Book 2: Betrayed

Guardians Of The Round Table- Young Adult Fantasy LitRPG

(Co-written with Storm and Rhys Petersen)

Book 1: Dexterity Fail

Book 2: Goblin Boots

Book 3: Singed Feathers

Book 4: Frog Mage

Book 5: Crystal Mine

Book 6: Cursed Harp

Rosie's Rangers- Young Adult Western Steampunk

(6 book series)

Book 1: Justice

Book 2: Vengeance

Book 3: Treachery

Book 4: Accused

Book 5: Wanted

Book 6: Corruption

Mark Of Kings- Children's Fantasy

(Upper middle grade/preteen)

(4 book series)

Book 1: The Arena

Book 2: The Island

Book 3: The Assassin

Book 4: The King

STAND ALONE SERIES

Demon Hunters- Young Adult Urban Fantasy/ Horror (with elements of romance)

Book 1: Blood Sacrifice

Book 2: Retribution

Book 3: Tainted

Book 4: Premonition

Book 5: Cursed

Book 6: Feud

Book 7: Extrication

Plea Of The Damned- *Young Adult Urban Fantasy/Paranormal*

(6 book series)

Book 1: Forgive Me Lucy

Book 2: Forgive Me Aiden

Book 3: Forgive Me Jena

Book 4: Forgive Me Kobe

Book 5: Forgive Me Marti

Book 6: Forgive Me Dawson

Realms Of The Fae- *Young Adult Urban Fantasy* (with elements of romance)

The Sword (short story in Like A Girl Anthology)

Heart Of Stone

Book 1: A Debt Owed

Book 2: Marked By The Hunt

Book 3: The Magic Collector

Book 4: An Unexpected Betrayal

Book 5: Imprisoned By Iron

Fairytales Retold (Short Stories)

Snow-White And Rose-Red

The Twelve Brothers

The Light Princess

Beauty And The Beast

Sleeping Beauty

Aschenputtel

The Golden Bird

The Frog Prince

The Death Of Koshchei The Deathless

Myths And Legends Retold (Short Stories)

Ion, Son Of Apollo

Sir Gawain And The Maid With The Narrow Sleeves

Princess Ilse, The Giant's Daughter

YOUNG ADULT NOVELS

Young Adult Fantasy (with elements of romance)

Elf Sight

Earth Bound

Young Adult Urban Fantasy

Stone Warrior (with elements of romance)

The Jungle Inside

Young Adult Contemporary (with elements of romance)

Through Your Eyes

The Ugly Stepsister

Perfect Little Princess

Young Adult Contemporary/Paranormal

Whispers In The Dark (with elements of romance and same sex relationships)

Over Too Soon (with elements of romance)

Young Adult Sci-Fi

Experiment X-One-Six (Urban Sci-Fi/Superheroes)

An Endless Dawn (Post Apocalyptic Sci-Fi)

CHILDREN'S BOOKS

Dragon Lord (Preteen/early teens) (Fantasy)

The Irish Wizard (Upper middle grade) (Urban Fantasy)

SHORT STORIES

Urban Fantasy

Eternally Late

Dealings With Joe

Glimpses (short story in That Moment When Anthology)

Contemporary

The Brat Next Door

Fantasy LitRPG

(Set in the same world as Guardians Of The Round Table Series)

Tales Of Inadon 1: The Disc (Co-written with Storm and Rhys Petersen) (short story in Game On! Anthology)

Post Apocalyptic Sci-Fi

Compulsive Directive

NONFICTION

A Year Of Weekly Writing Exercises (Creative Writing)

Cooking For Families With Allergies (Cooking) (Co-written with Storm Petersen)

Tell Me A Story, Grandma (Memoir)

For the most up to date details on available titles visit:

www.avrilsabine.com/books/bibliography

Disclaimer

This is a work of fiction. Names, characters, businesses, places, events and incidents are either the products of the author's imagination or used in a fictitious manner. Any resemblance to actual persons, living or dead, or actual events is purely coincidental.

www.ingramcontent.com/pod-product-compliance
Lightning Source LLC
Chambersburg PA
CBHW050752190726
48285CB00005B/1633